They've Escaped Out Of His Mind!

By Roger Davenport
Pictures by John W Taylor

They've Escaped Out Of His Mind!

By Roger Davenport

Pictures by John W Taylor

Bloomsbury

First Published in Great Britain in 1996
Bloomsbury Publishing Plc, 2 Soho Square, London W1V 6HB

Copyright © Text Roger Davenport 1996
Copyright © Illustrations John W Taylor 1996

The moral right of the author and illustrator has been asserted
A CIP catalogue record of this book is available from the
British Library

ISBN 0 7475 2682 6

Printed in Great Britain by Cox & Wyman Ltd, Reading

10 9 8 7 6 5 4 3 2 1

Chapter

In the topmost turret of Castle Cawnor, in the chamber that was her retreat from affairs of state, Princess Gloriana looked up from her tapestry. Her fingers, usually so nimble, were stumbling as for the fourth time she re-wove the silken figure of a Knight of Witherfall. The tapestry was to depict the history of the Dark Age of

5

Fortrain and it seemed the second Dark Age would be upon them before she finished another six feet.

She wondered aloud, "When will he come? Without him all Fortrain is lost."

"Lady, be patient."

It was Master Grievant who had spoken. Gloriana was not surprised, for wizards are wont to come and go unannounced.

"I speak sooth, Master Grievant. We are lost without Prince Bramnoc. The Destructor is massing his forces even as we speak. There is only one who may gainsay him."

Master Grievant spoke softly. "I am here, Lady. To serve you unto death if need be."

Gloriana stitched on mournfully. "You are old and your cunning fails you."

"By no means."

He threw back his heavy green cloak from his arm and pointed the Staff of Elroy at the tapestry. The Knight of Witherfall was at once made whole and in perfect proportion, but had mysteriously shed his armour and was completely naked.

Gloriana surveyed the botched magic.

"No man has travelled the Twelve

Islands as widely as you," she whispered. "You are wise and faithful. Yet your powers betray you."

All of a sudden she stood, her long neck taut with desperation, the pale hair shaken loose from beneath the golden crown. "Be a true sorcerer. Let a wind come and on it bring me Prince Bramnoc and every stout-hearted man and beast that follows him. Do this for me, Master Grievant, and your rewards will be great."

The wizard hung his head. "Lady, I cannot."

At this point the train crossed on to another line and shook the book so that the words blurred. Tom Short looked around vacantly at the real world: his mother, sitting opposite reading a magazine; fields and telegraph poles moving backwards outside the thick windows . . . How much more vibrant was the world of Fortrain! He found his place on the page and the real world receded again.

A hundred leagues distant from Cawnor,

beneath the lowering branches of the Forest of Grimthorne, Snorth the Dwarf, Son of Jax, beckoned impatiently to his bosom companion, Marblehead.

"Here. Set him down here. We are beyond pursuit and few would brave Grimthorne as the sun sets. The motion is opening his wound — quickly now!"

The ogre stooped a long way down, lowering to the dark earth the limp figure of Bramnoc, struck down within mere days of learning of his royal blood: blood which now leaked from him fast, staining the fine mesh of his chain-armour tunic.

"How can the Captain fight the poison of a Phraton spear?" Marblehead growled abjectly. "Even one as strong as I would sicken unto death."

Her face dirty and tear-stained, Little Bess spoke what all felt. "He mustn't die. It cannot be!"

Ahead of the little band was Mother Gamp. Her practical nature to the fore, she was already arranging a pallet of bracken which she scattered with pine needles for the fragrance they exuded. "Our Captain *will rest easy with that in his nostrils," she remarked when she had made the bed to her satisfaction. "The smell of the forest is the breath of life to one such as he."*

Tom raised his head again, breathing in through his nose along with the heroic Captain. Time for a break, maybe. This was the third time he had read *The Mirror'd Lake* and he was rationing himself to make it last. Of the whole series it was just about his favourite – the one where Prince Bramnoc finally found out about his royal lineage and realised his destiny. And of course it was one of the most exciting because in it the forces of Good were at their smallest and most in danger of extinction.

Thinking about the drama of it almost had him back in the book, but then he remembered the next bit was one of the slower passages. You knew Bramnoc had not been mortally wounded – not really – and now you had the serving-girl, Bess, being instructed by Mother Gamp in the use of woodland herbs. Bit tiresome, that.

He'd wait till he got to Grandpa's.

Mrs Short looked up from her magazine. "All right, darling?"

There was that sort of loving anxiety to her tone and she had said the word "darling" very much louder than was either necessary or desirable. Tom muttered "Mmn", meaning "fine", and again looked out of the window of the two-coach country train. He had hoped to make the journey to Marshton by himself, but it seemed his parents would never admit he had reached an age where such adventures might be considered. As an only child, he was in danger of continual embarrassments.

On the first train they had travelled in today, he had not felt brave enough to ask for food from the buffet in case his mother should afterwards whip out her handkerchief, spit on it and grind his face clean. It had been years since he had been assaulted in this fashion but he remained on his guard in such matters. She had little concern for his dignity.

"Tell you what, folks, we're almost there now. We're what you might call deep in his territory!"

Ahead of Mrs Short and her son was a party of Americans. From their intermittent conversation he had gathered that they were heartily appreciative of their trip to Europe; all except the one who had most recently spoken, a disapproving-looking woman of about fifty who wore a lurid pink tracksuit.

"Look at the land round here," said an old man Tom couldn't see. "Those fields have been there for centuries!"

"Yeah," said a big woman wearing dungarees. "It's the kinda place you'd get inspiration, all right."

"Old."

"Very old," she corrected him.

"Well, anyway – you can just sense how, living here, his imagination could embrace a whole fantasy world of legend. . ."

"It's the lack of civilisation. No distractions." This again from the pink tracksuit.

"I don't think you should criticise the country you're in, Phyllis."

"I wasn't." But Phyllis was clearly the complainer of the party. "And just why is it we can't see over Marshton Manor? You come all this way and you don't *see* anything."

"Private property, I guess. Don't they say that an Englishman's home is his castle?"

"A good tour operator coulda got us in there," Phyllis insisted. "I wanna see the room where he worked – it was my *dream*."

Tom had started to smile to himself. They were talking about C. M. Furnival, author of the Fortrain books. Tom's grandfather, with whom he was going to stay, had been Mr Furnival's gardener-cum-driver, and Tom had the firm intention of seeing the great man's house himself. It was the one reason he had felt happy about coming here and a part of him sympathised with Phyllis, who had travelled such a long distance and would be denied the privilege. Tom understood just how she felt – to see Marshton Manor would be to get closer still to the books, somehow. Even if no one was there.

As it happened, Marshton Manor was more heavily populated today than it had been since its pomp in Jacobean times.

In the overgrown garden of the low stone-built house, overlooked by its dark mullioned windows, Captain Magnificent, known as "Cap", gestured to one of the Grey Men to come to where he sat in the faded deck chair, regally indifferent to its accumulation of encrusted bird droppings.

His blond hair flopped attractively into his eyes and he shook it back with a peremptory flick of his handsome head. "Look into my eyes. . ."

The Grey Man squatted obediently in front of the low chair, hitching up the knees of his sharply creased grey suit as a businessman does when he sits. His blank, pallid face became even less animated as Cap fixed his brilliant blue eyes on him.

After a few seconds the Grey Man lost some of his definition as he became more vacant still. Thereafter he quite quickly began to become transparent, so that through him Cap began to make out the yellow of the dandelions in the long grass.

Gloria, lovely as the dawn, came over from the shade of the cherry tree and looked down fondly at Cap. Her American accent had improved over the weeks but was not yet perfect by any means and Cap found it just the slightest bit irritating.

"Great party trick, honey. Now let him be."

Cap sighed. "I am their leader. They love me. They would die for me." He raised his voice. "All right – that's all for now."

What was left of the Grey Man twitched and he began to regain solid form. "I'm so sorry, Cap," he blurted. "Thank you – I must have been dropping off just then."

He wandered away, shocked at his brush with mortality, and Cap sighed again.

"I'm bored, Gloria."

"I know you are, sweetie, but don't take it out on them. We haven't got an endless supply, you know."

Graceful as always, she knelt beside him, putting her heart-shaped face to his, mingling their golden hair in the August sunshine. Young and in love with themselves, they made a handsome couple; Glo-

ria in her floaty, pale-blue evening gown and Cap in the tight jeans and white blouson shirt which made him look like a latter-day duellist.

"I want those traitors *found*, Glor."

"Honeybunch, it's a great line, but it doesn't get us anywhere."

"Please. As a favour – could you speak English? Or, to put it another way, could you not do your American? Because you're hopeless at it."

"You leave my accent out of it. It suits who I wanna be. And speaking of English,

15

yours is sounding weirder every day."

Cap compressed his lips angrily. Since seeing a black and white film of *Robin Hood* on television and then later a simply thrilling movie called *Captain Blood*, he had begun to style himself on the long-dead movie star Errol Flynn – reckless, dashing and with a tenor voice which was just a little precious to the modern ear. He said in his freshly clipped manner, "I am surrounded by incompetents! *I want the traitors found*."

Gosh. That sounded dead on.

Gloria stroked his lean features fondly. "Mr Jackson and Marbles will get to them some time. Where can they hide?" She added in a less reassuring tone, "And don't call me Glor. It's Gloria – remember? I already shortened it once. Glor sounds so cheap. . ."

Captain Magnificent hardly heard this. He was setting his jaw at a determined angle and imagining it must look pretty good. It had been wonderful to become Captain Magnificent at the naming ceremony . . . though he could not help thinking things had not gone so well since. But his day would come.

It always did.

The train eased into the station and Mrs Short took down Tom's suitcase. As she did, she rammed his T-shirt back into his jeans at the exact moment Tom stood up, so that he sat down again rather suddenly.

The summer heat hit them on the platform, where Grandpa Blake waited in his corduroy trousers and check shirt, with his white hair and fierce tangled eyebrows.

"Travelling light, I see," he said sarcastically, taking the big case. It would have been heavier still, but with all the business of moving house Mrs Short had not given her full attention to burdening her son with things he had no use for. Grandpa winked at Tom by way of greeting and then said gruffly to his daughter, "Everything going all right? I'm sorry you've got to turn straight around and go back."

"I must. I don't trust the removal men one inch. It's awfully good of you to have Tom."

"Happy to help. Let's just get the case in

the van and we'll come back to see you off."

They walked to the car park with Tom trailing along behind them. "You wouldn't catch me moving house again," said Grandpa.

"Really? But now Mr Furnival isn't employing you, what is there to stay for?"

"My garden . . . the peace and quiet here."

Mrs Short said, "Of course it is stressful, moving. You wonder if it's the right decision . . . A bit frightening, really."

Her last words reminded Grandpa of something. "And how are the nightmares, Tom? All gone now?"

It was another of Mrs Short's failings, to tell all and sundry of one's private terrors. "Just about," Tom lied. The truth was the dreams were worse than ever. At least once a week he was threatened in sleep by an unseen horror more real than reality.

"It's all the books he reads," said his mother. "If it's anything to do with everyday life he doesn't want to know. I blame your friend Mr Furnival." She continued, not wishing to offend Grandpa, "How is he? Does he ever write?"

"Letters? Or books? Neither, as far as I know. He hasn't been in touch since he left the country. Well, that's C. M. Furnival for you. Lives in a world of his own."

At this moment, another being who used initials to preface his name was looking over the wall into old Mr Blake's garden.

"Roses, sweet peas . . . and the grape-vine. This is it. Everything as described."

J. M. Travesty-Warlock put into motion his long, ungainly legs and strode to the front of the house, which stood by itself several hundred metres from the village. Looking around quickly, he saw no one in the vicinity; the road was clear both ways.

He rang the doorbell and waited for a minute. It was clear old Mr Blake was not at home. When he looked round again, he saw coming from the village a business-man in a smart grey suit. The listless manner of the man alerted J. M. Travesty-Warlock to his identity and he edged around the front of the cottage, keeping as

close to it as possible, before slipping through the side gate into the garden. There he hesitated. Though the Grey Man was moving slowly, he would be passing the cottage soon, and the garden fence was low . . . J. M. Travesty-Warlock made for the shed by the compost heap. Since he had no sense of smell, he was unaware of the odour of the compost heap or the acrid smell of creosote coming from the dark wooden walls of the shed. All he knew was that it was dark and safe, if dirty, and that the hazy blocks of light coming through the window should be avoided if he was to escape detection.

With creaking knees he lowered himself down to sit beside the rusty mower. J. M. Travesty-Warlock was not hungry and was prepared to wait a very long time if necessary.

Back inside the station, Grandpa was double-checking the train times from the notice board. Though Mrs Short knew her route precisely, he was not convinced of her ability to look after herself, and Tom saw he was pro- tective in the same way his daughter was with Tom. The critical difference was that Grandpa could no longer lay down the law about what his

daughter did or did not do. All Tom wanted was just a little freedom, just to see what it was like. . .

By the ticket window, two men were talking to the station manager. One was very tall and wide and the other was wide and short. 'Tall' wore blue overalls; 'Small' had on a hairy green tweed suit. For want of anything better to do, Tom edged over to listen.

"An old bloke," Tall said in a slow bass voice. "Long white hair."

"Tall, sort of gangly. Well over sixty. Got a beard," the shorter man prompted in lighter, quicker tones.

"With a woman and a girl and a. . ." The big man in overalls stopped speaking, unsure of how to go on. Tom guessed he was not very clever. "A . . . er, and a. . ."

The short man helped him out. "And a pet," he said firmly.

"I'm sorry, I can't help you. We've had a lot of people through today."

"Very distinctive people. Large woman – "

The station manager interrupted the smaller man. "I can't help you."

The two men turned away without noticing

Tom. The very large man had a face like an oblong slab of stone, cut through with slits for eyes and for his mouth, which pursed up small in the middle as he looked at Grandpa's back. "Look, Mr Jackson," he said as quietly as he could in his booming voice.

The stubby Mr Jackson was even hairier than his suit, with a red beard which appeared to start almost at his eyebrows and crinkled its way down into a spade-shape. His eyes were bright and cheerful.

"Doesn't matter," he said softly. "It's not as if he knows us."

Grandpa turned round. "Shall we wait here or on the platform? It's cooler here."

Mrs Short said helplessly, "You really don't have to wait at all."

Grandpa said, "Nonsense."

Tom was still looking at Mr Jackson and his companion. Wasn't there something the faintest bit familiar about the two of them? Going out, they kept their heads turned away from Grandpa, though he had shown no interest in them at all. Tom was glad when the men were gone.

Chapter

Mrs Short's train was in sight by the time Grandpa thought of a topic of conversation for them. He said cheerily, "I've got a dreadful headache. I never used to get 'em, but recently it's like I've got one permanently. And I'm getting the oddest dreams."

Mrs Short was at once keenly concerned. "Why didn't you say before? You should see a doctor."

Grandpa's reply was minimal. "I would if I ever did, but I don't."

"But will you be all right with Tom?"

"Oh, yes. Shouldn't have mentioned it really. Sorry. We'll be fine, won't we, Tom?"

"Yes," said Tom politely.

"Oh, dear," said Mrs Short, suffering that kind of super-worry you get when you can't do a thing about the thing you're worried about.

Grandpa made it worse for her. "Ow," he said loudly, over the sounds of the arriving train, and he put his hand to his head.

Somewhere deep in the folds of Grandpa's mind the first of the Lancaster bombers, *B, Boxer*, trundled to its take-off point and lumbered down the runway, engines coughing and spitting like a tiger with a heavy cold. The night sky was overcast and it was chilly on the dank Fenland aerodrome. Lady Stephanie Gamp started the engine of the jeep and waited while Bess clambered in. Bess was small and her boots were heavy with mud, and the icy metal of

the jeep combined with her rough woollen RAF uniform to made the manoeuvre uncomfortable.

"No darts tonight," Lady Gamp said as they swept round to approach the buildings of the bomber squadron. "That's one thing I'm certain about. I don't care if I never throw another dart as long as I live."

"You've got to do something while you're waiting," Bess said. One of the runway lights illumined the two unlikely mechanics in the jeep and she saw that Lady Gamp was beginning to grow a definite moustache.

"Travesty-Warlock is a disgrace. Getting us into this."

"He'll get us out, I know he will. He's not like he is in the books. You can trust him. I do, anyway."

"It's too ghastly for words, being stuck in some old man's memories," Lady Gamp said, fingering her upper lip thoughtfully. "I never realised how depressing war was. Real war, that is. Hanging about for whole nights to see who's coming back from slaughtering Germans. It's always the nice ones who don't make it." She shifted her bottom on the hard seat.

"We'll be out soon. Nothing going's to happen to us," Bess comforted her.

"It'd better not." Suddenly Lady Gamp pulled the jeep to a skidding stop and lifted herself up, feeling in her back pocket.

"What's the matter?"

Lady Gamp pulled out a short-stemmed briar pipe and held it up with dismay. "Oh, no! Now I'm smoking. I'm going to kill Travesty when I get my hands on him."

Tom looked out through the dirty wind-screen of Grandpa's ancient van, where the sun still shone on the bustle of the village high street. It seemed unusually busy. Some Japanese tourists wearing bright clothes and broad smiles photographed each other in front of the amber-coloured stone houses, and at least ten businessmen were out and about, staring in a strange way as if they had come out of a cinema and still had the film going on in their heads.

"Is something happening here?" Tom asked. "All these men in suits. . ."

Grandpa turned his head a little, keeping his eyes on the road. "They opened this motel last year, with what they call a mini-conference centre. I don't know which is worse – businessmen or tourists." He winced and faced front again as his headache returned. "It was C.M.'s fault. He sold off a couple of fields he owned. A few years later we got the motel."

"I wish he'd write another book. I've read all of them – twice," Tom said.

"His publisher doesn't want any more. Well, he was getting old. They said he'd lost his touch, but it's probably just that the world's moved on and the books haven't. Do you know, he was thinking about the Land of Fortrain for twenty five years before he even started writing the first book in the series? Gave his life to Fortrain, he did." Grandpa sounded grimly satisfied.

"It doesn't seem fair," Tom said. They turned left into Grandpa's road and he added casually, with that very special pilgrimage in mind, "Do you still look after the house for him?"

"I pop in from time to time, but I'm not getting paid any more, so I don't do much. I was in there yesterday, as it happens. Thought I heard people talking – some village lads, most likely. They have a dull life here. So will you, probably."

Grandpa's cottage was small, dim and comfortable. Dim because the windows were small and he used only low-wattage light bulbs, and comfortable because crammed into the available space there was a wealth of battered, sagging furniture. Grandpa smoked a pipe and was lighting it now, after supper, and the smell mixed with the scent of ash from the fireplace.

There was no television and the silence

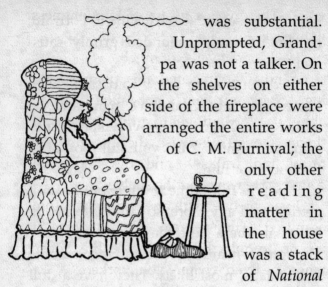 was substantial. Unprompted, Grandpa was not a talker. On the shelves on either side of the fireplace were arranged the entire works of C. M. Furnival; the only other reading matter in the house was a stack of *National Geographic* magazines in the lavatory. It was Grandpa who had introduced Tom to the Fortrain series, sending him at least one book for every Christmas and birthday. Other than this ritual they had had little contact except for the time Grandpa had come for Christmas, when he had found it all too rushed and noisy.

He cleared his throat and said, "Well." Once the word was out he waited until it had time to go round the room twice and be drawn up the chimney with the smoke from his pipe. "Not bored already, are you?" There was a gleam of knowingness in his eye.

"Well . . . not yet. Not much."

Grandpa appreciated this plain speaking. "Sorry, but there's not much I can do about it. We might get to a film one day, if there is one, otherwise there's only the radio and walks – and the books, of course." He waved at the shelves.

"I've got one with me, actually," Tom admitted. "They're great." He hesitated. "If it's no trouble, I'd like to see the house where he lived – where you worked."

"Yes, we can go to the Manor, if you want." Grandpa smiled at him; and then, with the beginnings of a friendship established, went on, "I don't suppose you know why your mother wanted you here any more than I do."

"She just said about keeping me out of their hair, with the move and everything."

"Troublemaker, are you?" It was light-hearted question but Tom was serious in his answer.

"No. I don't think I am." He was regretful that this was the truth. All his life he

31

had been told to be careful, when he wanted to break out, to be daring, to be . . . irresponsible. But there was obviously no chance of that here. His mother and father could hardly have found him a safer, duller environment. He sensed that Grandpa knew this too and was in some adult way embarrassed by it.

Breaking the silence which had returned, Tom asked, "What's Marshton Manor like?"

"Small, for a manor house. Old, damp, crumbling a bit. The heart's gone out of it now C.M.'s gone. We had our best days when he was still flying – game for anything, he was. Used to do buzz the village in the old Skyhawk. I can tell you they were glad when he packed *that* in."

Tom smiled at the idea. "C. M. Furnival used to fly around here in his own plane?"

"Oh, yes. The two fields he sold were part of his landing strip."

"A Skyhawk . . . Is that a Cessna Skyhawk?"

"That's right, Tom – made by Cessna and better known as a One-Seventy-Two."

Grandpa was pleased at this knowledge about flying. He had been in the RAF in the Second World War and had never lost his interest in aeroplanes. "Did I tell you that's how we met – C.M. and me – because of flying? We joined a bomber squadron on the very same day in 1944."

Tom did know this. When he did talk, Grandpa tended to go on about the war and had made everyone feel sleepy that Christmas with his verbal memoirs.

Tom asked, "Did you ever fly the Sky-hawk?"

"Oh, no. I was ground crew. C.M. was the pilot. Just like in the war. But he wasn't too safe up there. Always had his mind on those books of his. It got worse and worse. Had to forget about flying eventually."

Tom was about to ask more questions about Mr Furnival when Grandpa put his hand to his head. "Ow! This is too much. I've never known anything like it. I'm going to take a pill and go to bed. You don't mind, do you?"

"No, of course not," Tom said, in the gathering gloom. What else could he say?

The atmosphere in Marshton Manor was much more dramatic. C. M. Furnival's sombre dining room, with its heavy oak furniture and brocade curtains, was afire with light. A chandelier hung sparkling from the low-beamed ceiling, yet its many reflecting diamonds were muted in the uprising of brilliance from all the candles Gloria had strewn about the room, in candlesticks and saucers and even cups. She had lit every candle she could find and she had found a lot. Her lighting plan was designed for a glittering social occasion, but on the long table there was no food or wine to catch the yellow light from the pewter candelabra, which warmed instead the solemn faces inclined towards the head of the table, where Cap sat, with Gloria standing behind him, lovely as the dawn.

Gathered here were Mr Jackson with his huge friend Marbles and the remaining Grey Men, some thirty in all. Those who had survived thus far were those who had the greatest self-belief and their grey suits were subtly different, marking slight variations in character. The ones who had not found places at the table stood around the walls like so many statues.

At the far end of the table sat Des, dressed as a motorbike rider in black, studded leather. He had rarely been seen during the time they had been here and tonight it had been a surprise to some to see how small he was. He claimed he was modelled on Napoleon. Much as the little emperor might have been at a similar council, Des was the only one who made an effort to appear detached, leaning back and looking sombre and unapproachable.

One of the Grey Men had propped himself up against the doorjamb. It was obvious he was abandoning the fight for life, for his body was becoming translucent and from time to time altered its shape in sudden expansions and contractions, like a figure in a hall of mirrors.

Cap was speaking. "It's not good enough. Between you you've covered the whole village. Someone must have seen them. Where else could they be?"

Tonelessly, a large Grey Man sitting at the table said, "If they were hiding, how could we have seen them?"

"Because they've no more friends in the village than you have. Therefore, they could only hide in a place where you too were free to go. Or are you all morons?"

Another Grey Man spoke up resentfully. "You didn't even go looking! Stayed here on your backside all day."

Cap fixed him with a burning look, but before he was tempted to go further Gloria stepped forward, carefully placing herself in the maximum amount of light so that her long blue dress shimmered and her eyes shone.

"Hush, everyone. Hush. I, Gloria, lovely as the dawn, entreat you to remember that we gathered here are allies – friends. Can we not behave as such?"

Cap said dismissively, "Can it, Glor. And don't try the uplifting dialogue because you can't do it without help. 'Lovely as the dawn' . . ." His lip curled.

There was a nasty rasp in Gloria's voice. "At least I didn't call myself Magnificent and then mess things up all the time."

From his end of the table Des at last spoke up in his oddly deep, throbbing voice. "There is a solution to all our problems."

All heads turned to look at him and he continued, rising a short way until he was standing, "Give me an army of Grisemen and I guarantee – "

"Oh, shut up, Des, will you?" Gloria said with feeling. "You're a busted flush and everyone knows it. You get your own room and all you do is sulk in it. The only plan you ever have is to give orders to an army of Grisemen or Phratons – which we haven't got. What I say is, power corrupts and infinite power corrupts infinitely and any more power than *that* and you can't even make a cup of tea any more."

Des, the Great Destructor, was hurt. He said pathetically, "I was only suggesting – "

"Well, don't!" Cap barked commandingly. "Now can we all keep our heads? Assuming Travesty-Warlock doesn't have powers he's kept hidden from us, he can't go anywhere because he doesn't have any money." He took a plastic rectangle from his pocket and brandished it like a tiny dagger. "I have the one current credit card we found. And only I can imitate the signature. In this world you can go nowhere without money."

Gloria went back to her place at his side and Des sat down again slowly. Cap breathed deeply and went on, "That means that he and the others are still in the area. Now what we're going to do is go through all your reports again in more detail and if that doesn't get us anywhere, we start the search all over again."

Mr Jackson said brightly, "Don't bite my head off, Cap, but even on foot they could be miles away by now."

"With the M to drag along with them? Don't be daft, Snorth."

Mr Jackson tried not to sound offended. "It's Jackson, Cap. Son of Jax. I don't ever want to hear 'Snorth' again."

"I don't blame you. What I mean is, the M is pretty conspicuous and, as for how far they might have got, well, we've got two cars here. Actually, I wouldn't mind a go behind the wheel of the Rolls-Royce."

"Can you drive, Captain Magnificent?" a Grey Man said humbly.

Cap grinned in that attractive, boyish way he put on when he wanted to charm or win friends. "I don't know, but it certainly would be fun to find out." He tried a devil-may-care chuckle and it worked rather well.

Then they got back to business.

Lady Gamp marched towards the aircraft hangar situated farthest from the mess. It was almost too dark to see, but in her imagination the bowed structure seemed to bulge with the terrible might it contained.

The guard outside scrunched a glowing cigarette end under his boot and prepared to indulge his curiosity once again.

"Password?" he asked formally.

"'Mayhem'." Having assumed the title of 'Lady', she felt increased assurance. "Now stand aside."

"Go on, tell me. Why's it only you two who've got clearance? What is it in there? Secret weapon?"

"Something like that." She brushed past the man and entered the hangar.

The feeling of menace in there was quite palpable and her doubts were resolved: the creature was undoubtedly unsettled in this world and was swelling by the hour. Looking like a pale, pulsating slug the size of an airship, it was pulling steadily at the ropes that restrained it, which had multiplied, she noticed.

She called into the darkness, "Bess?"

After a second her young friend came towards her out of the shadows. Bess's inner energy at this moment was such that she was brighter by far than her surroundings.

"Hi, Stephanie. I've had to run more lines over it, to hold it."

"I can see."

Bess was grinning. "What a game!"

"I wish it was."

"We'll be all right. Just remember who you are."

It was their catch phrase, the difference between life and death, invented by J. M. Travesty-Warlock: "We must look after each other and we must *never forget who we are*."

Grandpa's spare room was the boxroom and there were the boxes to prove it. One of them, an old tea chest, acted as a bedside table and on it Grandpa had thoughtfully placed a lamp. Had he been more thoughtful he might have put in a brighter bulb; as it was, Tom had to lean over to the dim light in order to read in bed. As a token gesture of freedom from parental rules he had not undressed yet, though to spare Grandpa's bed linen he lay on top of the threadbare counterpane.

He opened *The Mirror'd Lake*. Yes, Mother Gamp making the bed out of bracken . . . the bit about woodland herbs . . . After that, Bess fed the wounded Prince Bramnoc.

No, this wasn't the best section of the book at all – now there was a long passage where they all argued about the advisability of moving on as soon as possible. He ploughed through every word dutifully. As usual Mother Gamp had a lot to say for herself; she was always fussing, just like a real mother, and always so boringly practical. If she wasn't making a bed out of bracken, she was making a tasty soup out of it. . .

He fell asleep with the light on.

In the garden shed J. M. Travesty-Warlock stirred for the first time in hours. Not that he had been asleep. He had watched darkness fall and had waited, crouching, in dead silence until it had been dark for a long period of time and the moment seemed right to him.

Now. He got up and, with precise, balanced steps, negotiated the obstacles between himself and the door.

The moon was shining brightly. A danger, but all the same it was wonderful to see that he had a shadow, which traipsed behind him across the little lawn. It was still a miracle to him that he was solid enough to make a shadow as he passed.

In the boxroom, Tom was having the dream. Once again he had been left alone at night, by chance, in some quite unremarkable place, in this case a railway waiting room, and once again he had the certain knowledge that there was no one within miles. There was, however, company of another kind. With mounting anxiety it became clear to him that the Thing was somewhere in the waiting room. . .

Probably under the bench on which he sat. The Thing was more real than reality and more frightening, because never seen. This time it would have him. He seemed to hear some kind of vibration. It was about to manifest itself, perhaps flowing up to smother him. Yes, here it came.

He woke.

For a moment, in that confused state between sleep and full consciousness, where dream is reluctant to give way to the physical world around you, he had the ultimate terror, because there *was* something vibrating somewhere. Just for a second . . . Then it stopped and he began to breathe again without realising he had held his breath.

And then the vibration came again, just for a second. There was a sound with it now, and it was Grandpa's doorbell.

Grandpa's doorbell, being pressed at intervals and only for the shortest of times. As if quickly and lightly.

Tom got out of bed.

Chapter

3

The house was unfamiliar and Tom could not find the light switches in the dark. Grandpa's room was just beyond the little bathroom, which smelled of some masculine hair preparation. He pushed open the bedroom door, which was already half ajar, and whispered, "Grandpa...Grandpa...?" It was odd how, at night, you felt you should only make just enough noise to wake someone.

Downstairs the bell rang again. Grandpa did not stir in his high, narrow bed and Tom could hear him breathing regularly.

"Grandpa!" Tom was reluctant to go over and wake him physically. Yet again the doorbell sounded, short but insistent. Whoever was out there, Tom wanted to answer the door himself. He felt suddenly brave as he tiptoed to the stairs and went down them as fast as he could. Who would the caller be? A policeman? Had something happened to his mother or his father – or both? Or was it an old friend of Grandpa's, drunk, maybe? Or someone who was somehow . . . dangerous?

The front door was solid wood and as Tom came near it the bell burst into sound one last time, making him jump. There was a chain to take off and the Yale lock was stiff or had a trick to it. When the door finally opened, it came with a rush and a gust of night air.

In the darkness the figure standing there was alarming in silhouette. A man. Tall, slightly stooped, and with long, white hair.

For his part, J. M. Travesty-Warlock was,

if anything, more disconcerted than Tom.
He was completely unprepared for an
encounter with a young boy, who said
rather sternly, "What do you want?"

"Good evening. I do hope I haven't disturbed you."

The old man intended to sound quite normal but, unable to see his face, Tom was not reassured. The voice was breathy, as though its owner had asthma or some trouble with his vocal chords. It was a sound like the sea in a shell, Tom thought later.

The voice breathed, "I was, er, I had hoped to see Mr Blake?"

"He's asleep. Are you a friend?"

"Oh, yes. But we don't know each other. Um, not formally. Or, to put it another way, not . . . at all." This was not going well, J. M. Travesty-Warlock feared. "We're not friends as such, but I'm extremely friendly." Even to his own ears this last sounded distinctly sinister.

Tom's hand was fumbling around for the light switch by the door. When he found it and pressed it, they both jumped a little, revealed to each other.

The boy was small and dark – and not stern, but frightened. J. M. Travesty-Warlock had no idea what to do next.

Tom could now see his visitor's face. Gaunt, white-bearded and with faded sea-green eyes, it had a defeated kind of charm; it was not in the least threatening.

"You'd better come in, hadn't you? I'll tell Grandpa you're here."

"Well, as matter of fact, it would be quite perfect to leave him sleeping. It would make my business with him so much easier. . ."

Now you could see him, the gentle, apologetic appeal in the old man's eyes robbed his words of menace. He wore a crumpled white linen suit which was too big for him, and a blue check shirt with a rust-coloured tie. Now he took out a little wad of papers from his breast pocket and, peeling off the top one with difficulty, said, "My card."

The piece of paper had been cut to the

> ## J.M. Travesty Warlock Esq.

size of a visiting-card and on it was written in a careful hand, "J. M. Travesty-Warlock, Esq." There was no address; nothing but the peculiar name.

He said, "You can trust me. I don't want to harm anyone."

"J. M. Travesty-Warlock," Tom said slowly.

"Yes. And you are?"

"Tom Short."

"Now that is a good name," J. M. Travesty-Warlock said with enthusiasm. "Brief and to the point. I wonder . . . You see, I do rather regret my nomenclature. It says it all, as far as I'm concerned, but after hearing you say it like that, well, you've confirmed what I've been thinking for quite a few days now. And we've watched the television – marvellous instrument, you see so much of the world and what it's like – and I would very much appreciate your opinion on something more up to date!"

"Sorry?" Tom said, lost.

"I wish for a better name." Remaining courteous, J. M. Travesty-Warlock changed the subject. "Can I come in? I'm extremely anxious not to be seen by certain people."

"Oh. Well . . . all right."

With a long, positive step, J. M. Travesty-Warlock came past him into the hall and Tom shut the door. When he turned, the old man was beaming at him with youthful, eager eyes.

"'Travis'!" he said. "That's what I've been thinking of. What about 'Travis'? It's good, isn't it? Strong and simple?"

"Are we talking about your name?"

"Absolutely. What d'you think?"

"Nothing wrong with it, I suppose," Tom said, bewildered.

"There isn't, is there? So: 'Travis' it is. That is a big weight off my mind – it's most good of you to help in this way. Where do we go now?"

"Go? Oh, um – the sitting room?"

"Why not?"

In the sitting room Tom found the light switch immediately, in time for his visitor to stride in after him without falling over the soft furnishings.

"Would you mind saying the name again?" said the being who had been J. M. Travesty-Warlock. It sounds so right!"

"Travis."

"Yes, that's the one. Travis. A great relief! Well, now – to business. . ."

Then Travis, as Tom was henceforward to think of him, stopped speaking just when it seemed he had much more to say and took a wander round the room, taking everything in. He glanced at Tom every now and then with a friendly smile, while he pondered how to go on. The books beside the fireplace caught his eye and he went over to read the titles of each one, nodding and smiling approvingly. Finally he asked, "Do you read?"

"A bit. I've read all those, anyway."

"I'm so pleased. And the gardener – your grandfather – does he like them too?"

"I'm not sure he's even read them. He

doesn't seem to read anything, really."

"I see. . ." Travis looked serious and thought a little more and then looked at Tom again. "Would you say it's true that the young have no fear?"

"Um . . . no. I mean – that's just me, maybe."

"Now that is a pity. Courage is such an asset when there's trouble abroad. Do you have a favourite character in these works?" He waved a hand at the C. M. Furnival books.

"Lots of them." Feeling that more was required, Tom volunteered, "I like Prince Bramnoc."

Travis was not impressed. "Oh. Well, I suppose one's meant to. You wouldn't think much of him if you met him."

"I don't want to be rude, but are you all right?"

"Better than that. Oh, much better than that. I exist. I am alive." The old man raised his fists in the air and shook them like a conquering footballer. "Travis lives!"

Tom started to back slowly out of the room. This had gone far enough. He

wondered whether he could shut the door
on this name-changing man and lock him
in. Or just run to Grandpa? Or to the
phone?

"Don't go, Tom Short."

Tom went slower, but continued back-
ing out.

"Do you have an interesting life?" Travis
asked shrewdly.

"Not specially."

Travis held up his hand just as Tom had
his fingers on the door handle. "And how
about imagination – do you have that? Do
you see the characters you read about? Do
you see . . . Master Grievant!"

As Tom was about to turn and run,
Travis's shape went transparent. It shimmered and spread like uncooked egg
white, and re-formed. There, taller than
before, was the same old man, wearing
now a deep-green gown with symbols on
it and holding a wooden staff in his hand.
He said, "I want your help, Tom Short,"
and his voice was full and authoritative.

Tom was terrified. Seeing this, Travis
reversed his egg-white trick and reshaped

himself back to what he had been, sunny side up, smiling encouragingly. He said in his wispier voice, "What a shock for you – I am sorry. I've got to get a move on, though, because I rather believe time is against us."

Tom said, "Who are you?" in an unstable voice.

"Travis. That's who I am *now*. A.k.a. Master Grievant." He added helpfully, "That means 'also known as' Master Grievant."

"I know what a.k.a. means," Tom said with asperity, "I knew *that*. But if you are Master Grievant, how did you . . . how come . . . how did you . . . *how*?"

"We got out," Travis said with innocent satisfaction.

"*We*? There's more of you?"

"Of course. Why else would I be here?"

The candles were burning low. "Go over it again."

"This is just bullying, Cap," Mr Jackson said wearily.

"Where did you go then? After the post office?"

"We went to the station. He wasn't there."

Marbles said in his gruff voice, "We did see the gardener bloke. He was there with a woman and a boy."

"And it couldn't have been them in disguise?" Gloria put in. "Travesty-Warlock can change his appearance, remember."

"You couldn't feel him being one of us. I'd stake my life on it."

A very mild-mannered Grey Man said softly, "They weren't in the pub. People eat crisps there and drink the muddy water." He added proudly, "I was there quite a time. No one noticed me at all."

"Yes, so you told us. It's not something I'd boast about, personally – being completely anonymous," Cap said morosely.

Slumped by the door, the Grey Man who was fading raised his hand. "You haven't asked me what I did," he whispered pitifully, anxious for just one moment in the spotlight before he himself declined to zero. "I saw the gardener too."

Des looked up at his end of the table.

"Cap, I'd like to ask this man a question," he said in a tone which promised masterly cunning.

"OK, Des. I'm bored with this anyway."

Des looked at the see-through Grey Man and thought for a moment. "Where?" he asked cleverly. "Where did you see him?"

"Oh, brilliant," Cap said, disgusted.

"He went into his house," the Grey Man whispered. "I was with Travesty-Warlock when we overheard him describing his garden when he was talking to the postman that day, so I knew it was where he lived. When he went in, I looked, and it was the right garden."

Mr Jackson was puzzled. "He got about a bit, didn't he, Mr Blake? He wasn't with the woman and child?"

"He was alone. It was what they call 'T' time – four o'clock."

Mr Jackson said calmly, "They were at the station dead on four o'clock. How close were you when you saw him?"

The Grey Man by now could hardly be heard and could hardly be seen. "Not . . . very. . ."

"It was T-W!" Mr Jackson realised.

"Went into the house, did he?"

"That's . . . that's what I thought he did. . ."

Cap rose to his feet. "He's still there. Travesty-Warlock enlisted the gardener's help somehow. I'd guess he got him to smuggle the others into his cottage. That's where they all are!"

Mr Jackson said kindly to what was left of the Grey Man, "You've been very helpful."

Glad that he had not lived in vain, the Grey Man disappeared completely, outlived in the air by his grateful last words, which lingered eerily.

"Thank you. . ."

Marbles said sadly, "Tragic, isn't it?"

"No time for sentiment," Cap said crisply. "We need a plan of attack and the keys to the Rolls-Royce."

"Not the Rolls, honey," Gloria cooed. "Too conspicuous. The estate car will take more of us in any case."

"I want to drive the Rolls-Royce," Cap said, outraged. "I am Captain Magnificent – he doesn't drive around in a thing you go *shopping* in!"

The ensuing argument about this, and then about the strategy needed, took up a little time.

"You're telling me that the Destructor is now a real person, living in Marshton Manor?" Tom had almost worn out his amazement by now, though he was prepared to believe all the old man was telling him. Because he wanted to.

"Des – that's what he chose to be called when we had our naming ceremony – he's the least of our worries. It's Bramnoc you've got to look out for." Travis was grim, sitting in Grandpa's chair by the fire.

"But he's a hero!"

"Only to himself. I'm afraid all that 'aren't you wonderful' stuff has turned him into a narcissistic megalomaniac. He gave himself the title of Captain Magnificent and no one's got the strength of character to put him straight about things. Princess Gloriana – 'Gloria' as she now is – she actively encourages him, in the most awful American accent. Don't think I didn't try to make them see sense."

"And Snorth – the dwarf – who's he, then?"

"Mr Jackson." *Of course*, Tom thought. "Wanted to dress as a racecourse book-maker for some reason. And Marblehead is Marbles. They always made a double act, if you remember your Fortrain."

"But . . . you say you 'got out'. How?"

"I don't want to waste too much time on this, but since I'd now like your help. . ." Travis got up from the chair. "You see, we all knew, when Mr Furnival read the letter. From his publisher. We knew we were going to be . . . discontinued. You've got to understand what it's like living in some-one's mind . . . Information of all kinds is charging around. Everything he reads, for instance, sort of floats around – and our Creator is a voracious reader. You get to know a lot. And characters from other books come and go too, though they're a bit like the Grey Men – not as certain of them-selves as we are, not as three-dimensional. Oh, dear. It's awfully hard to explain."

Tom struggled to understand the concept. "You're alive in there – as the characters?"

"In a fashion. If your creator has been working with you for a long time, you do develop an identity. But the scenery – one's surroundings – well, it's not like here. In there, you've no idea how vast it is, and where you are and who you're with is always changing, without any logic to it. You can be talking to a friend and the next moment you're somewhere else with someone else. . ."

"Like a dream," Tom thought aloud. "Like living in a dream?"

Travis was pleased. "Yes, as far as I'm able to judge, much like a dream. You're doing well. Now, then. We were aware that we had some fame, some status in the world outside, and we didn't want to be forgotten. The Creator was very upset too – he actually became physically ill. I've always felt close to him, because I believe that I am partly modelled on his less confident self, and when the channel appeared . . . We were having a conference in a house – "

"A house in his head?" Tom was confused.

Travis elaborated. "A place we all knew.

It was where Furnival grew up, so it was often in his thoughts. Everything was very disturbed because he had this high temperature. And from somewhere in all the things he'd read and thought, I knew there was a channel out. And that day there was a hole in the air – that's the only way I can describe it. I'd never seen it before. I asked, and those who wanted to get out put their hands up. It was rather moving . . . And so I led them out – I went first."

"How?"

Travis said, "I jumped from the roof. There had to be a gesture of supreme courage, you see. They all saw me disappear, so they followed. It takes the most enormous self-will, but the ones who escaped were up to it. We came out through his mouth. The legend is, 'In through the Eyes, Out through the Mouth.' Don't ask me where it comes from. We hid. He was so ill he was taken to hospital and, when he was better, he went to convalesce in another country. We didn't know he'd do that. We wanted to talk to him, eventually."

"'Out through the Mouth'. . ."

"That's the way. But the willpower doesn't stop there. You have to have a continuous belief in yourself. Not all of us have. The Grey Men. . ." He shook his head. "Poor, lost creatures! There were sixty or so of them when we started out. Characters who were never wholly formed in the Creator's mind, but who wished to live. None of them will last. But while they do, we're seriously outnumbered."

"Who is? Who's we?"

"Well, you and me, and Stephanie Gamp – that's Mother Gamp to you – and little Bess, the serving-girl. And one other. . ."

"Who's that?"

"I should have known it would follow us. When you think of the books, who or what is the most powerful single being in them?"

"Well – it's not you," Tom said honestly.

"No, I'm afraid not. I never liked it – the way I was always portrayed as an incompetent man of magic. Hence my original choice of name. No, not me, and not Bramnoc, and not the Destructor either. . ."

For a reason he could not place, Tom

remembered the nightmare he had dreamed earlier. A thought began to well up in his mind. . .

Travis prompted him, "Where did the Destructor get his power from? What was it that he kept hidden throughout all the books, despite our best attempts to locate it? What lives in bottomless pits or beneath deep seas, where only he can reach it?"

The thought came spilling out. "The Monorath," Tom said.

A chill ran up his spine like a spider in a hurry.

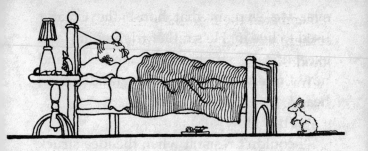

Chapter

Travis appeared to go off at another of his tangents as he said, "Where exactly is your grandfather's room?"

Tom was reeling with the information he had been given. "It can't be true about the Monorath! The Monorath can't be here! He's – what's it called – the embodiment of all evil!"

"Well, it is a *little* worrying. He just happened to be at hand when we made the escape. One didn't come across him much when we were 'inside' – if you follow me – but he was always lurking around whenever we were in that house the Creator used to live in. He's rather frightening, and exceptionally stubborn . . . and . . . and now I'm afraid he's in your grandfather's head."

"What! How?"

"I couldn't resist it when the idea struck me," Travis said helplessly. "It seemed such a good hiding place. Your grandfather was there on one of his occasional visits. It wasn't uncomfortable for him . . . The, er, 'transference' took place when he was in a deep sleep, which I was able to induce. He wouldn't remember a thing about it – don't worry!"

"And that makes it all right, does it?"

Travis was hurt that Tom could not see it from his point of view. "Well, I'm sorry, but I had to stick the Monorath *some*where. Bramnoc wants to let him off the leash, and if he did, then I very much doubt we could control him. . . " He thought of something that might make the boy feel better about it. "Bess and Stephanie are in there with him, so he should be all right. They befriended him, you see, and he's as good as gold with them."

Strangely, this news did not make Tom any happier. "So you're telling me that a strange girl and a woman and the ultimate power of evil are in my grandfather's head?"

"That's it. You've got it." Travis smiled at him gratefully. "Though heaven only knows what it's like for them, swimming around in a stranger's imagination! Now, where's your grandfather's room? I've got to get them out."

The estate car was not smart, but it was big. It was also old, and getting older by the second with Cap behind the wheel.

His knowledge of driving came mainly from car-chase sequences on television. One headlight was smashed already, where he had just hit the gatepost when

leaving Marshton Manor. They had found a trailer used in the big garden and in it were crouched six Grey Men. The journey was exhilarating and had already charged their self-belief to a high level, causing them to radiate a pale phosphorous aura of brightness.

Shining hardly at all but equally moved by the adventure were Mr Jackson and Marbles, who had elected to travel on a rusty bicycle they had found in one of the outhouses. Marbles sat on the seat holding on to Mr Jackson, who sat on the handlebars holding on to the side of the trailer. They had suggested taking the Rolls-Royce as well as the estate car, but Cap had been fixated by the idea that he should be the only one with the glory of steering a high-velocity motorcar. He sat crouched over the wheel like a young child in a frenzy of concentration, with Gloria (secretly still lovely as the dawn) by his side and another five Grey Men crowded together uncomfortably on the back seat with Des the Destructor. The thought that they should be inconspicuous had been either abandoned or forgotten about in the soaring drama of the moment. They had, after all, been cooped up in Marshton Manor for a very long time.

In the motel close by, the disgruntled American woman, Phyllis, was standing by the window in her bedroom, still wearing her pink tracksuit. She was finding it too quiet to sleep. Phyllis lived in New York in an area where there was always noise and movement, and this kind of peace spooked her. It was unnatural, she thought. Therefore it was with something akin to approval that she saw headlights wavering madly on the road from Marshton Manor and heard the tormented squeal of car brakes.

In the light from the MOTEL sign in the gravel driveway she was able to see a large car career by, dragging a trailer full of men and a two-manned bicycle. The road curved here and the bicycle developed wheel-wobble and broke away from the little procession. With only one place to go, it raced into the motel driveway as the car and trailer sped onwards. The larger of the two cyclists applied the brakes and the smaller man shot off from his perch on the handlebars and landed on the gravel just before the bicycle too hit the ground, throwing off his companion.

Amazingly, they were neither hurt nor shaken by their mishap as far as could be seen, for after only a couple of seconds of whispered consultation they set off again, only this time with the larger man athwart the crossbars and the smaller man pedalling, unable to see a thing behind his passenger. Though small, he was powerful, for in no time the bike was back on the main road and heading again for the village.

Lucky for some, Phyllis thought to herself. Out having fun when there's no one about!

And the thought made her think some more.

In the cottage, Travis had placed Grandpa's bedside light on the floor before switching it on, at pains not to wake the old man. He had assured Tom that his grandfather would not be damaged or distressed by the removal of his inner guests, but privately Tom was so thrilled by the situation that he would not have minded if Grandpa had suffered very slightly.

"The sanctity of the individual is paramount to me," Travis announced pompously in his whispery tones as he lowered himself to kneel near Grandpa's head. "If your creator had continually made a fool of you in his books you would share this philosophy. Now: utter quiet, please." And to Tom's amazement he began to sing, softly and melodiously, "'When I'm calling you – ooh ooh ooh, ooh-ooh-ooh . . . Say you love me too – ooh ooh ooh, ooh-ooh-ooh. . .'"

"What's the point of that?" Tom asked incredulously.

"Please don't interrupt. It's the 'Indian Love Call'. A cracker of a number, if you're in love."

"Oh. Are you?"

Travis sighed. "'Love is the sweetest thing . . . the something and the neatest thing . . .' That's another love song . . . Yes. Over the years I have developed strong feelings for Stephanie Gamp. Though I must confess to having doubts about her choice of 'Stephanie'. Can I get on now?"

"Yes. Sorry. But what's the point of it – singing?"

"I am summoning them forth. It was our prearranged signal." Then Travis resumed singing.

"'When I'm calling you – ooh ooh ooh, ooh-ooh-ooh . . . Say you love me too – ooh ooh ooh, ooh-ooh-ooh. . .'"

Grandpa opened his eyes. You could see he was still asleep, for there was no expression in them. Travis stopped singing and waited. Grandpa's mouth dropped open as if by command, like a drawbridge, with mechanical precision. Then Tom saw what Travis had meant by 'a hole in the air', for around Grandpa's mouth there was an unfocused circle like a thin mist. . .

"Hi!" said a girl's cheerful voice coming from Grandpa's mouth, and Grandpa breathed a loud "Aaahh!" Suddenly Bess was standing beside them, grinning, more comfortable now she was out of her RAF uniform and back in jeans and baggy sweater. "Brilliant!" she said to Travis and then looked at Tom. They were the same height exactly. "And who's this?"

"Boy called Tom. Are the others coming?" Travis asked urgently. The hole in the air still lingered round Grandpa's mouth.

"Should be. Unless Steph's having trouble with it. She told me to go first." Bess looked around the room, interested in her new surroundings. Her tone changed when she said, "And who's *that*? Oh, no!"

Grandpa's curtains were not fully shut and between them a faintly glowing face could be seen through the glass.

"Cap!" Travis exclaimed and instantly transmogrified into Master Grievant, rushing to the window in a swirl of robes with his staff held aloft.

"Boo!" he said loudly.

Outside the cottage, the pyramid of Grey Men which supported the spy at the top wavered when Cap recoiled from the window, and went for an uneven walkabout as the three biggest Grey Men at the bottom attempted to keep their living tower upright. It was a vain effort: the structure swayed, buckled and toppled. Cap hit the ground first and the rest fell on him.

"My darling!" Gloria screeched. "Are you hurt?"

"Geddem offamee," Cap's muffled voice came from beneath the heaving grey pile of bodies.

In Grandpa's bedroom Travis was a man of action – or rather, a wizard of action, for he still presented himself as Master Grievant.

"Nowhere to hide! We'll have to make a dash for it – quickly, while they're confused." As he spoke, he gathered up Grandpa as easily as if he were an eiderdown and lifted him on to his back.

"What about Steph and the thingy?"

Bess shouted as they ran for the stairs.

"She must be having trouble with him. The main thing is that we hold on to the gardener. . ."

Without being told one way or another, Tom followed them, his heart beating wildly with the exultation of total recklessness.

On the front path Cap's face emerged from the scrambling pile of bodies. "Surround the mouse!" he seemed to shout, the last word distorted by a Grey Man rolling across his face.

Des had skipped nimbly into the porch when the living ladder collapsed, and now skipped back again hastily as Travis swung open the front door. While Cap struggled to his feet, the Grey Men hesitated; as Master Grievant, Travis was an imposing figure.

Cap yelled, "Get them!" and Travis raised his staff majestically.

"Avaunt!" he cried and then strode through Cap's little army with the pyjama-clad Mr Blake still on his back, followed by Bess and Tom. Once past the last of the staring Grey Men and out through the gate, they broke into a run, going round the estate car and the trailer only to confront Marbles and Mr Jackson arriving on the bicycle.

"Stop!" Marbles bellowed at Mr Jackson and they tumbled from the bike as it skewed sideways. Marbles recovered himself and held out his huge hands in a threatening welcome.

"Come to Daddy. . ."

Behind them Cap had led the Grey Men into the road. There certainly were a lot of them. "Or you can come back here if you like," he said, and smiled his reckless smile.

Tom could not understand why Travis was dawdling. "Use your powers," he urged.

Travis said briefly, "I haven't got any, Tom. Sorry."

Grandpa lifted his head, which dangled down by Travis's chest. "Would someone kindly tell me what is going on here?" he asked, dazed yet fierce. "Let go of me!"

Travis politely lowered him to the ground. "I'll have you charged with assault!" Grandpa said, so outraged that he did not comment on Travis's appearance.

"Grab them – *now*!" Cap shouted.

Grandpa and Travis were the main targets for Mr Jackson and Marbles and also for the troop of Grey Men. Bess snatched Tom's hand and pulled him away as the two old men were engulfed by their foes. Mr Jackson darted out a hand for them but missed and then had to tackle Grandpa.

Bess said rapidly, "Can you do anything with this?" She indicated the bicycle.

"Yes." No time to boast that he was pretty good on a bike.

Behind them Gloria was screaming, "Get them in the car – we gotta get outa here!"

As Tom wobbled away with Bess perched lightly on the crossbar, there was a great heaving and grunting around the car and the trailer, which were about to become even fuller than they had been on the journey here.

"You're good at this, aren't you?" Bess commented about Tom's skill on a bicycle.

"They're not following us, are they?" Tom panted.

"No," Bess called back calmly, "but they certainly will be, because this is the way to Marshton Manor."

Tom at once looked around. Back by the cottage the estate car rocked and swayed, but was not yet travelling anywhere. He pedalled on as hard as he could towards a corner which was coming up a couple of hundred metres farther on. Fortunately the car and trailer had to be turned all the way round before a pursuit could begin and Cap was unable to complete the operation by the time they swept round the bend. Tom kept an ear open for the car's approach – and had an eye on the hedgerows running beside the road. When he saw a gate he was mightily relieved.

In the car, Grandpa and Travis were half smothered under a weight of Grey Men, with Des on the top, his head touching the roof. Conversation between Cap and Gloria was intimate, since she was sitting on his lap as he drove.

"Travis isn't going to help you just because you caught up with him, sweetie."

"He doesn't have to. I saw how it was done. Heard it, too."

"Gee! You're a genius, honey."

"I'll tell you one thing."

"Yes, my sweet potato?"

"Next time we'll take the Rolls."

"Just you and me?" Gloria breathed.

"Well . . . Just you and me and Stephanie Gamp and the Monorath."

Gloria was less ardent. "Oh. Romantic." Then, "Where are they?"

"Who?"

"The kids – they went this way. So where are they?"

"Who knows? And who cares?"

"They could make trouble for us, couldn't they?"

Cap shook his golden head. "This isn't Fortrain. What could they do?"

"We could rescue them." Sitting behind the hedgerow in the field, with the bike and Bess, Tom was still on a high of excitement.

"You've been reading too many books," Bess said with a friendly kind of contempt. "It'd be dangerous."

"They didn't look too dangerous. Not any of them, really."

"They are. They don't obey your rules – they don't even know a lot of them. They'll do what they want, even if it hurts someone."

"And you're not like that?"

Bess did not immediately answer this. "We've only lived for a few months. We're . . . *new*. Me and Travis and Steph, we just want to fit in. The others aren't bothered by that."

"Well, what are we going to do? I'm cold." Tom shifted his position on the hard, lumpy earth. The excitement was dying down.

"What's it like, being cold?"

"Don't you know? Can't you feel it?"

"We don't feel temperature much. We don't eat at all, and we can't smell anything. . ."

She sounded depressed, so Tom said, "You're not missing too much. Well, there

80

are some tastes and some smells, even, that you'd like." To cheer her up he went on, "But you've got the best of it if you can see and hear."

"And touch – we can feel things. That's wonderful. There are so many kinds of. . ." She was stuck for the word.

"Textures?" Tom suggested.

"Yes. So many. And so many – what would you call them? – densities. I've never touched a person, though."

Tom held his hand out. "There you go."

"That's very nice of you."

She reached out and took his hand. He said, "You feel a little cool to us. Otherwise quite ordinary, I suppose."

In the darkness he could see she was smiling. "What is it?" he said.

She kept holding his hand, longer than he would have wished. "It's wonderful," she said at last. "We're not so different."

"Oh. I'm glad. I mean – if that's what you wanted." Managing to extricate his hand from hers, he said, "So what do we do? They've got my grandfather as well as Travis. I don't like it and I don't suppose he does, either."

"Yes, maybe we'd better try and get them away, after all. Only, Cap and Des, well, if they caught you . . . They've got this thing about power, you see. Can't get enough of it. I don't know much but I know it isn't good for them." She got up briskly, again bursting with energy. "Still . . . Come on, then! Let's give it a go."

Lady Gamp was worried. She sat smoking her pipe in the jeep, which was parked on the extremity of the airfield. They had just been bombed by enemy aircraft and fires blazed in the Sergeants' Mess and in the guardhouse. The water tower was down and the firefighters were up against it everywhere.

None of this bothered Lady Gamp especially. It was clear that the gardener in whom she was trapped was undergoing intense inner turmoil for some reason, causing these raging images. What concerned her was the effect it was having on her simple-minded companion. The secret-weapon hangar was quivering to the point where it must surely shatter soon. She had no idea why the escape procedure had been halted, but prayed that when their deliverance came, he would settle to one of his more manageble sizes.

She started the jeep and drove across the bomb-pitted runway towards the hangar. All she could do was to try to calm him down and hope for the best.

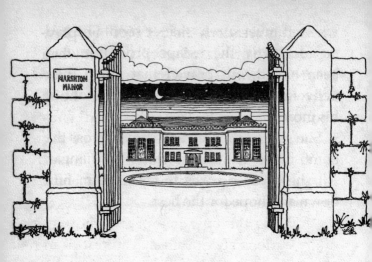

Chapter

5

Tom and Bess had biked on for some minutes when the chain snapped: it had been put under severe strain by Mr Jackson and Marbles earlier. So they walked on through the night towards the Manor; and talked. Tom learned a lot about the creations. He called them that to himself, because what else would a creator produce? It seemed that when C. M. Furnival was writing the books, his creations did his bidding, playing the hero or wizard or villain, but when his mind was otherwise engaged they were like actors with no work; they hung about together and gossiped, and journeyed through the wide world of the mind. True to his character in the books, Travis was the greatest traveller. Bess had a great deal of respect for him.

"He was the only one of us who was really curious about things. The rest of us were just happy to find we existed. A bit complacent, really. Except for Travis, you get a general rule that the bigger the character you have in the books, the bigger-headed you are. Even Steph likes to think she's a little bit grand. She's got this idea she's descended from – you know, related to – a character from Charles Dickens and that this makes her special, so when we had the naming ceremony in the Manor she added the 'Lady' bit. We didn't really think it out properly when we chose our names. I didn't bother with it at all. But I'm glad Travis finally decided to be Travis. He only had initials before – he never even worked out what they stood for."

"Bess isn't such a bad name."

"Thanks. Um, Tom. . .?"

"Yes?"

"You said Travis wanted your help. How?"

"I don't know. It was like he suddenly thought it'd be a good idea."

"Well, I don't want to seem rude, but I don't see what you could do to help him. He's got to stop Cap – he's going to take the Monorath to the man who publishes our books. If the man doesn't change his mind and let the Creator do some more, then Cap's going to let the Monorath kill him."

"Would the beast do that? Could he?"

"Travis thinks so. We've been keeping the Monorath nice and calm till now. He's not clever, but he's horrid if you get him upset. He starts growling whenever Des goes near him. And he starts to grow, too. Pretty scary."

"I thought the Destructor was his master."

"Only in the books. The Monorath hates him. Really, there's no knowing what the beast could do if he finds out how powerful he is here. . ."

They went on in a thoughtful silence. In Marshton Manor, Travis and Grandpa Blake sat staring at each other opposite C. M. Furnival's leather-topped desk. Ten Grey Men were their jailers, standing silently around the walls, quite happy to be of use and do absolutely nothing at the same time.

Grandpa Blake, having asked for clothes, wore a pair of his erstwhile employer's corduroy trousers and an old tweed jacket he had always liked the look of. The clothes were slightly too small and the slippers they had found for him pinched his feet, contributing to his bad humour. The whole house had a marvellous odour of mildew and antique wellington boots, but Travis couldn't smell it and Grandpa Blake was used to it.

Travis had found that the old man, who throughout his life had been untouched by fiction, art or imagination, was much less receptive than Tom to the story he had to tell. Travis had transmogrified for him, changing out of his wizard's garb, but Grandpa had only blinked and accused him of being a shifty sort of chap.

"Well," said Travis, finally, helplessly, "what *will* you believe?"

"You're some kind of madman who is putting a spanner in the works of a bunch of adventurers who've got some plot going against my old friend and employer, C. M. Furnival. That's about as far as I've got." Grandpa was smugly satisfied with this concise appraisal of the situation.

"You don't remember me from before? I was able to send you to sleep, if you recall. It was most gratifying – from my point of view."

"That's loony. I've never set eyes on you and I'd like to meet the man who could put *me* under."

"Well," Travis sighed, "at least you don't think I'm an enemy."

"You're a maniac, but you seem to be on the right side – that's all I could say."

"Well, fine. That'll have to do."

"I've got a terrible headache," Grandpa remarked.

Cap had opened the door quietly, looking for a dramatic entrance, and was happy to find one.

"Your headache will shortly be taken from you," he said theatrically. "Along with a couple of other unwanted items."

Grandpa was taken out. Four of the Grey Men went with him.

"I suppose if I were to tell you that you were on the wrong side in all this, you wouldn't let me go?" Travis enquired of those that remained.

The Grey Men looked at each other before one took the responsibility for answering. "We elected Cap as leader. We need a leader."

"But think of what he does to you from time to time!"

"It's all right for you. You've got a personality to hang on to. We have to get our security where we can."

Another of the Grey Men chimed in anxiously, "You won't try to make us vanish, will you?"

"There's too many of us, in any case," another sneered.

Travis said loftily. "You wouldn't understand, but all life is precious to me. Even yours."

Downstairs Gloria had rearranged the dining room to give another effect, that of an operating theatre. The lighting was subdued everywhere except over and around the centre of the room. The chairs had all been pushed back and Mr Jackson had even been able to find a green tarpaulin with which to disguise the table.

Held down on it by four Grey Men, Grandpa blinked in the light. He was surprised how strong these men in grey suits were. They looked so very docile.

"Look into my eyes," Cap said, leaning over Grandpa.

"Oh, not more of this hypnotism rubbish! The old fool upstairs blathered on about that."

"We share a talent our Creator had in a less developed form. Do you remember it was his party trick in the RAF? Only with him, of course, the subject had to be willing. Keep looking at me."

Grandpa was getting woozy. "Is it

Mr Furnival you're talking about? Yes . . . he did used to . . . a long time ago. . ."

Seeing he had become passive, Cap began to croon the 'Indian Love Call'. He was not sure of the tune, quite, but his ear for the words was perfect. "Say you love me too . . . ooh ooh ooh, ooh-ooh-ooh. . ."

The hole in the air opened very quickly. "Aaahh. . ."

Lady Gamp appeared in the room in an agitated state and in her chosen garb of a woman's black suit, which showed up perfectly the pearls around her neck. Stout and womanly and with not a hair out of place in her mauve-rinse coiffure, she sported a luxuriant ginger handlebar moustache. "Well, at last! Thank goodness! It distorts you if you're not careful, that kind of thing."

"Gee, honey – I understand what you mean." Gloria was horrified, but within seconds the moustache was fading and Lady Stephanie Gamp was restored to her full splendour. She became less flustered and looked about her.

She said, "Ah. So it's you, you swine, is it? Too bad – too bad. But we had to get out, so. . ." She glanced at Cap, who was still singing at Grandpa's mouth. "I knew it. It didn't feel right. Don't worry – he's coming. He was just behind me."

"Aaahh."

The Monorath was in the room with them.

As they approached Marshton Manor, a dim luminescence alerted Tom and Bess to the two Grey Men who guarded the gates. Tom pulled Bess back and they stepped down into the roadside ditch.

"They don't look dangerous," Tom whispered. "Just a bit bright . . . Couldn't we talk to them, or something?"

"They're devoted to Cap. And terrified of him. And they're very strong," Bess whispered back. "Actually, I think we all are, compared to you. It's something to do with the amount of willpower you need to stay alive."

They scurried back along the ditch to find another way into the house. This involved a staggering trot across a bumpy field, at the end of which they found themselves at the back of the Manor outside the orchard. A high wall ran most of the way around the property and here where it was darkest and dampest the wall seemed to be held together mainly by lichen. Apple trees stretched their branches over the top. Tom got a hand and toe-hold in the old wall, but it crumbled under his weight.

"Put your foot on my hand," Bess urged confidently. "I'll give you a leg-up."

As Tom found out a moment later, what she meant was a heave-up; one which sent him soaring, legs pedalling the air, straight to the top of the wall. Branches raked his face and he clung to them while he found his footing. "Ow!"

"Sorry." Bess went back and took a running jump at the wall, launching herself at it with a will. Her hands grasped the top, Tom grasped her hands, and a second later they stood together looking through the leaves towards the dark old house.

"Have they gone already?" Tom wondered.

"Could have. But Cap likes to get the maximum drama from everything and that takes time . . . Hard to know until we take a look." Bess jumped down into the orchard without so much as jarring herself, it seemed. "Want a hand?"

"No, I'm all right." Tom climbed down very cautiously, chagrined by both her strength and her daring. They made their way through the apple trees, occasionally pulping an ageing windfall under their feet. The leaves had just begun to turn and some drifted down through the night air, alarming Tom when one brushed his cheek.

"Quietly," Bess said. She had the ability to tread almost soundlessly, without going below a walking pace. Then, "Stop."

A dimly shimmering form was walking lethargically along the path which ran round the house. As Tom and Bess made themselves as still and narrow as possible among the trees, another Grey Man came from the other direction. The two shiny businessmen went by each other without acknowledgement.

"That's a pity. Makes it hard if he's got them everywhere," Bess commented when the Grey Men had gone around their respective corners of the house. "Now: run!"

Tom followed her as she raced towards the building. Reaching the path, she leaped over it so as not to make a noise on the gravel. Tom joined her, panting. On this side of the house there was not a single light to be seen.

"Where's the back door?"

"We're going in through the basement. Here."

She pointed out a wooden hatch on a boxlike shape jutting from the walls. Looking around rapidly, in case there were more Grey Men on patrol, she made a fist of her hand and punched right through the hatch.

"You *are* strong."

"I think you could've done it. It's gone

rotten." Bess fumbled with her hand through the ragged hole she had made. Finding the bolt she was looking for, she drew it and lifted what was left of the hatch, which sagged badly. "Jump in."

"It's all very well for you, but . . . how far is it?" It was pitch black; he couldn't see a thing.

"Just jump down!"

The tension in her voice decided him and he jumped, landing painfully on a pile of logs covered with plastic sheeting. He had not thought it could get any darker than this until Bess, sitting on the edge of the hatchway, lowered the door as far as she could over her head. Tom heard her muted call of "Watch out!" and rolled aside as she dropped in beside him, letting the hatch door slam shut.

"How did you know about this place?" Tom asked when the pain had subsided a little.

"We were looking for somewhere to hide the Monorath."

"Before you stuffed him away in my grandfather?"

"Yes – who we're going to rescue, if you'll shut up for a minute." She sounded cheerful, though. "Here, take my hand."

She led him through the blackness by memory and what seemed to be a kind of radar. Only once did they touch anything, when Tom's shoulder caught some shelving and bottles moved and clanked together.

"Stairs," Bess at last whispered. "Just feel your way up them."

She let go of his hand and tiptoed the steep staircase. Tom went up on his hands and knees, in a crouch. Oddly, he found it was easier with his eyes shut. At the top he bumped into her. He could hear her working on a squeaky door handle, turning it slowly, and asked, "Where do we come out?"

"Near the back stairs."

The door opened just a little. Tom saw that the darkness was not as deep out there. Bess put a warning finger on his lips and by degrees pushed the door to the point where they could slip into the dim corridor.

Tom could just see her jerk her head to

the left and they went that way. Over Bess's soft tread, Tom could hear faint rustling sounds of movement.

"Bess!" Tom stopped her. "I think – "

"Lights on!" came an exultant cry and the hall light snapped on, revealing at first only the glum-looking passage they were in, and then, as he came round the corner, the leather-clad figure of Des, followed by Grey Men. Bess turned to run but more Grey Men now stood at the other end of the corridor. They trotted in to cover the cellar door and all was lost.

"And Cap said I couldn't even manage a launderette – whatever that may be!" The Destructor's gratification was unpleasant to see. His mouth writhed with pleasure. "I knew you'd come skulking back here. Little Bess . . . and her little friend!"

In fact Des was only a couple of centimetres taller than Tom and Bess. "Binoculars," he went on. "Had a man on the roof. I thought of everything." He turned to the tallest Grey Man. "Take them!"

"OK, Des. Um – where?"

"To Cap, of course, cretin!"

They were hustled through winding corridors to the front of the house. Here there was a large stone-flagged hall opening on to the main staircase. All of a sudden, the door they were going to was opened and several Grey Men came out fast. From inside the dining room came a low, menacing rumble. Des's party came to a stop and Bess looked at Tom.

"I don't know what your grandfather's feeling like right now, but that's the Monorath and he's not too happy."

Des marched into the room importantly. There came a deep, shuddering animal howl and he came out again in a hurry, half pushed, half carried by Captain Magnificent himself.

"Are you mad? You know how he feels

about you! Leave him to Stephanie. Even she's having trouble with him tonight."

Tom gazed at Cap, Captain Magnificent, Prince Bramnoc of the House of Elwine in the land of Fortrain. Though he was not disposed to admire him, there was a lot to be said for his choice of name, since he undeniably cut a heroic figure.

Cap looked at the boy who was staring at him with his mouth agape, and dropped Des on the stone floor.

"You got the boy, too."

Des got up with the speed of the small man attempting to recover his dignity. "I got them both! Aren't you going to thank me?"

"Sure – thanks," Cap said casually. "Stick 'em with the magic man."

Des came to Tom and put a cold, hard hand on his throat. "Couldn't I torture this one? Maybe he knows something."

"His times tables? Some rudimentary biology? No, you cannot torture him. You can help Mr Jackson get the cars ready. When the Monorath is quiet I want to leave at once."

"Well, can I torture him later then?"

"I don't see why not." Cap went back into the dining room, saying, "Glor, where's the credit card? We'll need petrol."

Des fixed a burning stare on Tom. "Later. When I'm back. We'll do some biological experiments, you and I. . ."

Tom felt frightened and alone. Bess saw this and said, "You'll fall asleep one of these days, Des. Dreaming about all the horrible things you'd like to do. And then what'll happen?"

Des looked almost shocked at the thought. "Take them – and don't ask 'where' again!" he said and went to the front door.

The Grey Men bundled Tom and Bess into one of the other reception rooms, which turned out to be the study. Grandpa was asleep here on a leather sofa. Grey Men stood silent and watchful. Sitting behind the desk, Travis looked mournfully at Tom and Bess.

He said, "Now that *is* a pity. I was rather counting on you two."

Chapter

6

"I'm hungry," Tom said.

"What's it like?" Bess asked immediately.

They had fallen into a state of silent despair in the study, except for Grandpa, who was sleeping soundly and a little noisily beside Tom on the sofa. He had not woken since the 'operation'. Travis said this was quite healthy and nothing to worry about.

"What's it like," Tom repeated, trying to

define for himself the sensation of hunger. "It's like being anxious . . . empty . . . restless?"

"But I bet it's wonderful when you eat, though. We don't eat anything."

The guarding Grey Men, doubled in number for security, seemed to have gone into some kind of suspended animation. Only their eyes moved, eerily, from speaker to speaker.

Tom asked, "What's up with them?"

"Conserving their energy," Travis said. "If you think you're hard done by, think of them, Bess."

Tom got close to Bess where she sat on the floor beside Travis, and whispered, "I think they're going to fall asleep in a minute. We might have a chance then."

To his surprise Bess laughed loudly. One of the Grey Men stirred, shifting his position a little. Tom looked at Travis for explanation.

"If we fall asleep, we die," the linen-suited wizard said mournfully. "That is, we cease to exist. We have to be conscious of ourselves and who we are all the time.

For myself, I think it's a small price to pay."

After Bess's feats of strength Tom had been envious of the creations. Now he was not so sure. It was no fun at all to be hungry, but when you thought about it, eating even ordinary foods was one of the best things life had to offer. And as for never sleeping . . . Imagine. As it was, when he had a bad day he had the consolation that it was going to finish when he went to bed. To sleep – when you didn't get scary dreams – was like getting time off in between living. But to be conscious every hour of every day and every night; never to get a rest. . .

Outside the window came the sound of footsteps on gravel. Car engines started. More footsteps, some of them running; people calling in low voices.

"Poor old Cap," Travis said, rousing himself. "Hopeless business, this quest for glory. And someone's going to get hurt."

Two of the Grey Men wandered to the window. "He looks wonderful," said one admiringly.

"Magnificent," said the other. "And look at her. Lovely! Lovely as the dawn."

"Watch this. Here comes the Monorath."

Tom got to his feet and hurried to the window. Before the Grey Men dragged him away he just had time, in the light from the open front door, to see a good-looking young woman with an older, bigger woman, leading some kind of animal towards an ancient Rolls-Royce which was parked beside the estate car. The animal was of a light colour and the size of a large pig. That was all he had time to take in before he was shoved roughly back towards the desk.

"Did you see him?" Travis enquired kindly. "And was dear Stephanie with him?"

"I think so."

"That's something, anyway. What did he look like?"

"Well, not much." Tom was puzzled by the question. "Bigger than a big dog, but I couldn't really tell. I thought he would look . . . different."

"He can," Travis said simply.

They all listened to the departure of the two cars. The travellers sounded excited and there were a lot of them. Eventually the vehicles pulled away from the house and motored down the drive.

"Poop poop," Travis said softly. "Off into the unknown. I was saying: it is strange, this need for a kind of immortality. Wanting to be in more books, to be known by more people. Just to be sitting here, existing in actuality, seems so much more . . . so rich." He turned to Bess. "Did I ever tell you, young Bess, that, 'inside', the rumour is that one can get away for good? Live the life of an ordinary person?"

"You didn't tell me, no. But I don't see why not – if you've got the strength of character."

106

"There is even a legend that the immortal Mr Toad is alive and well and working as a mini-cab driver in the Baron's Court area of London."

"Oh, come on," Tom broke in. "Mr Toad? He's for young kids."

"Nevertheless, an incredibly powerful creation," Travis replied placidly. "But I can't think that many get out at all, let alone for good and all."

"Not Mr Toad, though." Tom couldn't believe it. "If you'd said a character from – I don't know – Shakespeare, I might be able to understand that."

"Ah, well, Shakespeare's something else again. There's another theory there: that his characters don't need to get out in the same way that we did. They have the ability to inhabit actors who play the parts. Or perhaps 'infect' is the proper word. Hamlet, Mercutio and King Lear are among the most virulent parts one can play, I'm told." He addressed a Grey Man. "Now: why don't you let us go? What harm can there be in it now?"

"We're not allowed to," the Grey Man

answered primly. "Cap said we were to keep you here. He said it was a matter of national importance."

Travis stood up, fuming. "You're pathetic! Spineless! Your beloved leader is set on causing every kind of mayhem and you follow him through every tortuous turn of his twisted mind! If only everyone had gone on with my plan, we would have achieved the desired goal eventually – and by peaceful means!"

"What was your plan?" Tom asked.

Phyllis's views on sleep were similar to Tom's. You needed a good rest in the hours of darkness. Without examining her motives fully, she told herself that a long walk might be tiring in the right kind of way. She felt more awake than ever as she rolled off the motel bed and reached for her trainers.

In C. M. Furnival's study, Tom picked up another of the carbon copies of the painstakingly typed letters. It read much as the others had done.

Dear Sir

Please please please, would you consider making a television series of the Fortrain books, by C. M. Furnival? All my friends and me think they're the greatest!

> *Yours sincerely,*
> *Billy Smith (aged 12)*

PS Prince Bramnoc is my favourite character.

When they arrived in Marshton Manor, the creations had a mission: to ensure that the Fortrain series of books would be continued. In the early days here, the creations had watched vast quantities of television and Travis had quickly absorbed the style and content of letters sent in to television companies. He grasped the importance of the visual media in the modern world and realised that if the books could succeed there, their future would be assured. His idea had been to flood every TV and film company with these fan letters.

Tom picked out another letter from the huge pile Travis had placed in front of him.

Dear Mr Goldman,

I have seen all your films and they are terrific.
My class at school has a big favour to ask:
Please please please could you make a film out of the Fortrain books (by C. M. Furnival)? We never stop reading them and we know it'd be a great movie – if you were the one who produced it!
Please please please!

Yours sincerely,
Laura Smith (11)

PS   Prince Bramnoc is my favourite character.

The postscripts at the bottom had been Cap's idea. He had insisted on them. Unfortunately, because the creations had felt it wise to use fake addresses for the fake children who were supposed to be writing the letters, they had no idea if anyone had replied, which was why Cap had lost patience with the scheme.

Now Tom said, "He could have been right – Cap. I don't know if you'd get anywhere with these."

Bess said, "It was a much better plan than Cap's, anyway."

"I still have faith," Travis said, disappointed. "The public is listened to. Why, all the time, on the radio, you hear how they're going to play a record requested by Gary Bayliss of Northampton. It seemed to me it was merely a question of sending out enough. With an infinite number of letters one's bound to get through to someone eventually. And the books are good – you said so yourself."

Tom shook his head. "Even so. . ."

Grandpa chose this moment to wake up in a bad temper. "Am I still here?" he groaned. Then, seeing Travis: "And are you still here?"

"Don't lose heart, Mr Blake. This is merely a temporary reversal."

"Still crazy as a fruit bat, I see. Hello, Tom!"

"Hello, Grandpa."

"They've kidnapped you too, have they? What's going on here?"

When Tom tried to explain, Grandpa dismissed him out of hand. He was a child, taken in by the madman Travis. Bess was another deluded child. What they had to do was to get the police on to this. Whatever these scoundrels were plotting against C. M. Furnival, it must be stopped.

"Grandpa, please believe me."

Travis sighed. "It's no good, Tom. You may find, as you grow older, that you too find it hard to take on new ideas."

Grandpa made a discovery. "Thank goodness – my headache's gone!"

Tom started, "That's because – "

"No, it isn't. I don't want to hear any more about it. Don't worry, I won't tell your mum and dad. They'd only make you see a child psychologist, and I don't believe in that kind of thing."

Travis fixed a kindly eye on Grandpa. "Mr Blake, you don't believe in much, do you?"

"I believe in my country," Grandpa said

belligerently. "I believe in fighting for what is right. Isn't that enough? That was why we joined the RAF, you know, me and Mr Furnival. You knew where you were during the war."

"Now *those* beliefs could be useful," Travis said with a glint in his eye.

It was only after Phyllis had jogged out of the motel grounds that she realised fully that she was going to Marshton Manor to fulfil her dream of seeing as much of it as possible. Well, of course she was! She accelerated to a brisk speed and it was hard for her to tell whether her heart was pumping so hard because of the exercise or the thrill of it all.

When she got there, the gate to the old place stood wide open. This was a welcome surprise. Even though she knew the place to be deserted, Phyllis did not jog along the gravel driveway but trotted instead, lightly, through the shrubs alongside. As Tom had found earlier, at night the instinct to be quiet is strong.

The Grey Man with the binoculars was

still on the roof, perched behind the crenellated parapet above the guttering. Cap and Des had forgotten about him and, with no new orders to obey, he still scanned the environs of the house. He had been lucky to spot the young people's approach in the dark and was delighted when movement again caught his eye.

As the figure paused in front of the house, the Grey Man saw, without any particular surprise, that it was a woman in a pink tracksuit. She tiptoed closer to the building and out of his sight. Feeling he would earn extra marks if he could direct the troops to her exact location, he leaned over the parapet to get a view of her movements.

Facing the front door, she stood still, suddenly doubtful how to proceed. She took a step towards the door and the Grey Man leaned farther out – and plummeted fifteen metres to the ground by her side, impacting on the earth with a terrible thump.

Phyllis screamed. A glowing businessman had fallen to his death from far above her. When he got to his feet, dazed but unhurt, and said politely, "Pardon me," she screamed again and ran for her life.

"Alarm!" the Grey Man shouted, chasing unsteadily after her. "Alarm!"

It described Phyllis's feelings exactly. She pounded round the corner of the house like an Olympic athlete and, as the Grey Man came after her, made for the front gate. He was an exceptionally strong runner and cut off this escape route almost at once, so she swerved back towards the house, skidded around another corner and fell straight through the rotten hatchway into the cellar.

She was lucky in that the momentum of her fall took her beyond the logs and down on a pile of cardboard boxes, which made a comparatively comfy landing. But, boy, was it dark in here!

In the study they heard the drama outside. Footsteps thundered through the house as the remaining Grey Men ran about in all directions. Almost at once Travis said to the Grey Men within the room, "Trouble. Interlopers – go and take a look."

They stayed where they were, so he rephrased it. "Cap would want you to deal with this. Your friends may need your help."

When they still did not respond, beyond exchanging stares of intense anxiety, he added, "I expect there'd be a prize for showing initiative and a nice sleep for failing to show it. . ."

This was a clincher, but it took the Grey Men a long time to make the decision on who would go to the aid of their comrades.

In the cellar Phyllis blundered about with the vigour of one who is drowning. If there was an object to bump into, she bumped into it. Finding some kind of stick within reach of her hands, she grasped it as a potential weapon. She collided with a variety of shelves; pots fell on her head, wine bottles shattered by her feet and cobwebs of enormous antiquity and density clasped her hair.

The door to the cellar was opened above her and she rushed towards the light, flourishing the stick. The sight she presented to the oncoming Grey Men was horrify-

ing in a very specific way. Charging up the stairs towards them, screaming incoherently, was a wild creature drenched in whitewash, with her face covered with black cobwebs like a veil and an old mop in her hand, which in their consternation they took to be a human head on a pole.

"A Phraton!" one of them gasped.

"A female Phraton! Deadlier than the male!" another wailed.

And they fled.

In the study, the Grey Guard was down to eight. They walked around in an agitated fashion as howls and screams echoed through the corridors.

Bess said softly to Tom, "I think we're going to get out."

Travis had the same feeling. He stared across the room to where Grandpa sat on the sofa with his fists clenched in case danger came into the room.

"Mr Blake. . ." Having got his attention, Travis thrust forward his head and stared at Grandpa even more intently. Grandpa found himself held by the green eyes and the rhythmic words Travis employed.

"I sense deep down you want to help us, and we are going to need your help. You are one who fights tyranny: now you are called to arms once more . . . I know you *want* to believe, so surrender your stubborn denial. I ask as a friend, a fellow fighter against dark forces. Help us without understanding if you will not see the truth, but help us you must. If you would deny me, raise your finger."

He waited patiently, while Grandpa continued to look him in the eye.

"I don't think it's fair, using hypnotism." Tom said.

"I'm not sure he is, exactly," Bess answered. "He's pretty strict about what you should and shouldn't do. It's part of who he is."

Grandpa did not raise his finger. When he heard frantic conversation and a high-pitched shriek nearby, Travis eventually broke their gaze, turning to the nearest Grey Man. "Did you hear that?" he remarked. "It seems Phratons are loose in the house. More than one, by the sound of it . . . Did you hear the shrill squeal of triumph after a kill? Distinctive, isn't it? I'd forget about us and save yourselves if I were you."

"We can't let you go – Cap would destroy us! What are we to do?"

Travis stood up, helpful. "I believe the standard procedure is to make a living shield of your hostages while you remove yourself to a safer environment."

Then Grandpa got to his feet too. He

looked almost exuberant, for Grandpa. "But be quick or we'll withdraw the offer!"

He and Travis exchanged a nod of understanding.

It was with gratitude that the eight grey, unformed characters took hold of their four prisoners and led them out into the hall. Several other Grey Men rushed by them, going upstairs. One of them did not make it. He was becoming see-through with terror and negative thoughts and collapsed, overturning an umbrella stand noisily.

"Phratons?" one of the guards enquired.

His fading colleague breathed, "I saw one . . . Oh, my word! Time to go." And he went.

Tom witnessed the vanishing with horror and pity, but had no time to dwell on it. Running swiftly towards them on her state-of-the-art trainers was the wild-eyed Phraton with her mop.

Bess screamed as loudly as anyone: Phratons loomed large on her personal list of horrors. Travis took advantage of the moment.

"We're doomed! Save yourselves – scatter!" he shouted. Reduced in numbers and grateful for orders of any kind, the eight-

man guard let go of their prisoners and fled in all directions except towards the terrible Phraton.

Which came to a sobbing stop. "Please, somebody, tell me," it gasped, "what is this? Is it some kind of motivational exercise or what? It's a salesman's convention, right? Why else would you throw yourself off a roof?"

Bess calmed down. "I don't think that is a Phraton," she said doubtfully.

"I'm an American," the Phraton look-alike said with tremulous pride.

And fainted.

Chapter

Bess said it was mean to leave Phyllis flat
out in the hall with nothing for company
but hysterical Grey Men, but Travis knew
they must make their getaway before
Cap's troops sorted themselves out. When
they were clear about what they had to do,
they were dangerous adversaries.

Quitting Marshton Manor, the escapees
hurried into the shrubbery to avoid being
sighted. Crouching there, Travis asked
courteously, "You have a van, do you not,

122

Mr Blake? I wonder if you could give us a lift to Oxfordshire?"

"What's in Oxfordshire?"

"As I tried to tell you before, a very foolish character is about to turn loose a creature whose idea of harmless fun is Armageddon. I – we – must stop him."

"And he's going to do this in Oxfordshire, is he?" It was wonderful how Grandpa had perked up with the prospect of active service. It seemed now to Tom that he had not needed so very much persuasion after all. Grandpa went on, "I'm afraid I couldn't recommend my van as a means of getting anywhere fast."

"They already have an hour's start on us," Travis said despondently.

Grandpa was positively flushed with commitment to his new cause. "C.M.," he said, "I mean Travis. Will you trust me?"

"I will, Mr Blake."

"Call me Arthur. This way, then."

The sight of the Phraton lying immobile on the floor did wonders for the confidence of the Grey Men, who gradually gathered around her in increasing numbers, so that when she came to she could well have been waking in the middle of a businessmen's convention.

"Hi, guys," she said weakly. "Game over?"

"What would Cap want us to do?" came a voice from the crowd.

"Tear her limb from limb?" came a helpful suggestion.

Another Grey Man piped up with, "I think we're meant to torture her first, but I can't remember why. . ."

"Speaking of remembering things, our orders were not to let Travesty-Warlock and the others escape."

"Oh. Have they? It wasn't *my* fault."

"It wasn't mine, either!"

"Oh no, I'm fading . . . Can we make up our minds?"

"If he's fading, say it was *his* fault!"

"That's not fair. Whose fault was it, anyway?"

A furious argument developed as the Grey Men tried to set the blame on each other. During this Phyllis crawled out between their legs and let herself out of the front door. One of the pairs of legs was becoming transparent, she noticed dully.

A few minutes later, limp and bedraggled, jogging very slowly back to the motel, she tried to rationalise her experience and failed completely. Over the next months she would review and embellish her memory of the strange events, telling with more truth than she could know that C. M. Furnival's house was possessed by spirits of the divine muse. She would become vague when pressed to describe their appearance. There is not much the imagination can do with a grey suit.

"Here we are. Now we stand a chance!"

Grandpa Blake spoke with pride. Looking at the building, Bess knew she had seen something very similar inside Arthur Blake's mind. Made of corrugated iron, it was a smaller model of the hangar in which the Monorath had dwelt.

"Would I be right in guessing there's an aeroplane in there?" she asked.

"Yes, of course!" Tom said. "How did you know?"

"Only an underpowered toy, but it's all we need!" Grandpa said enthusiastically.

Travis said thoughtfully, "And you can fly it, can you, Arthur?"

"I can get it started; after that it's up to you, C.M.! Like the old days, eh?"

"It's a magnificent plan, Arthur, truly a bold stroke, but I should point out to you that I am not C. M. Furnival."

"Oh. No. No, you're not, are you? Whatever made me think. . ."

"No, no. Quite understandable in its way – and flattering. I do share many of his characteristics."

"I thought it was such a good idea," Grandpa said, crestfallen.

Bess said briskly, "Where's the van, then?"

"Wait." Travis was thinking. "Yes. We'll take the plane. I have explored and absorbed much of the Creator's knowledge. In all likelihood somewhere in me is a modicum of flying skill."

"In all likelihood?" Tom heard a little squeak in his voice. "It's all right for you – you probably wouldn't be hurt by an aeroplane crash, but me and Grandpa, we . . . we break!"

"Then don't come. I'd rather you did, but if it worries you. . ."

The idea of reverting to his old cautious self was hateful to Tom. "No no. We'll come all right, only . . . only . . . be careful."

Using his unhuman strength Travis snapped off the padlock on the hangar doors. Inside, because of the sweep of its wings, it looked as though the little propeller aeroplane was welcoming them with open arms. The wings were fixed to the top of the four-seater cabin and supported by reassuringly thick struts thrusting up and outwards from the Skyhawk's belly. With no difficulty at all Travis and Bess pushed it out into the open and Grandpa searched out the keys and went to drag the fuel hose from the pump outside. Mr Furnival had thought of everything when setting up the ways and means for his hobby.

While the others kept a lookout for Grey Men, Grandpa filled the tank. Everything he did was informed with relish and excitement.

Tom said to Travis, "You knew he wanted some adventure, didn't you?"

"Oh, yes. Like you, Tom! Unlike you, he has his memories of the war, when he felt important and really alive. He'd like a bit more of that. We each have a golden age in our lives."

"Do we? Did you have one?"

Travis took his time in answering. "Not yet."

"Where do we have to fly to?" Tom asked. "I mean, do you know the address?"

"Mr Haines, the publisher, was one of the first people we wrote to. I researched him a little, since he's such an important figure to us."

Tom said suddenly, "I don't want to look like I'm putting things in the way all the time, but I think Grandpa's forgotten something."

"And what is that?" Travis replied equably.

"There isn't a runway for the aeroplane any more. Mr Furnival sold the land."

Travis said loftily, "Oh, don't be so faint-hearted."

Faint-hearted or otherwise, the prospective aviators would have stood little chance of any kind of escape from Marshton Manor, were it not that the Grey Men were still engaged in the heated business of apportioning blame among themselves. Not wishing to disturb this activity, the absconders hauled the areoplane bodily into the farthest corner of the field without starting the engine. Beyond the distant boundary hedgerow they could see the outline of the motel. It was a low building, but they would still have to be airborne when they reached it. . . .

The shouting from Marshton Manor got louder. The Grey Men had remembered their duty and had launched a search; a boisterous affair which included the wild yelling of such phrases as "Geddem!"

Travis said, "Hear that? Time to go."

Grandpa looked along the truncated length of the overgrown runway. "I'm sorry, everyone," he said, "it'd take a genius to get us up in time. Anyone got any other ideas?"

"Think of me as a genius," Travis said

and climbed up into the cabin.

The shouts of the Grey Men were louder, nearer. . .

"Those who want to come: get in," Travis ordered. "Now – this is the control wheel, is it?"

It was Grandpa who got in next, to help Travis. Tom and Bess climbed up to sit behind the old men. You could see in every direction through the windows of the cabin, even behind you, and Tom kept a lookout for Grey Men.

Travis stared at the controls and muttered rapidly to himself, "Throttle . . . trimmer . . . flaps. Fowler flaps, Arthur – am I right?"

"You do know something about it after all, Travis!"

"Yes . . . and here are the rudder pedals, but I don't seem to know how to start her up. Would you oblige, Arthur?"

"If you don't know how to start it, Travis, should you be attempting a take-off?"

"Yes."

A single shiny Grey Man saw the aeroplane as it began to trundle across the ground. It was the same Grey Man who had fallen from the roof. He let out a cowboy whoop and loped across the field.

In the cabin Tom shouted, "Here comes one!"

Travis said calmly above the noise of the engine, "I suppose it's a question of going as fast as possible as soon as possible and raising the elevators as late as possible."

"Well, that would be the theory, yes," Grandpa shouted back.

The Grey Man turned to whoop again, rustling up help, and put on speed. Three other Grey Men jumped the fence into the field in time to see their companion running alongside the plane. He got a hand on the door.

Inside the plane Bess yelled, "He's slowing us up!"

The Grey Man's grimacing face was less than a metre from hers. She twisted in her seat and held on to it tightly as with a savage kick she knocked the door clean off. The night air swirled in and the Grey Man disappeared behind them, still holding on

to the door. He turned a full somersault and bounced to his feet. They could just hear him shout in a manic scream, "I'm telling – I'm telling on you!"

In casting away the cabin door he hit another of the Grey Men and all four of them started arguing again.

Travis eased back the control stick as the Skyhawk reached the hedgerow and the aeroplane lifted a fraction, crashing through the tops of the branches. It wobbled and sank . . . and rose slowly into the sky.

"How about that?" Travis cried. "How *about* that!"

It was while Travis attempted a victory roll that Phyllis looked out of her motel-room window one last time. At last she felt close to sleep, but the sounds of an aeroplane engine had roused her. Twitching back the curtain and looking blearily out, she saw a Cessna light aircraft swooping at her, upside down. Before it skimmed over the motel she was able to see that one of its doors was missing.

Phyllis let the curtain fall back into place and staggered to her bed, making the mental note that she must holiday in Europe again next year. It was far more exciting than she had given it credit for.

In the aeroplane there was a fair amount of chaos. They had only just managed to strap themselves into their seats before the horizon flipped over, and coins from Grandpa's pockets were rolling round on the ceiling. Bess was clutching Tom around the shoulders as added insurance against his falling from the plane. Looking down, he appreciated the gesture. They carried on upside down, though somehow this felt less unusual than it might have, up here in the sky. With the cabin door missing, an erratic wind gusted around them.

"Wheeeee!" Grandpa shouted.

The Rolls-Royce swept along the deserted roads, followed by the estate car. "A convoy," Cap had called it.

Gloria was singing one of C. M. Furnival's favourite songs. On discovering that she knew it, she could not get it out of her head. "'She was only a bird in a gilded cage . . . A beautiful sight to see,'" she trilled.

"Can it and read the map," Cap said sourly. He was easily bored and they had been driving in a straight line for miles.

In the back of the car sat Lady Gamp and a Grey Man. On the floor beneath their feet lay the hard bulk of the Monorath.

The Grey Man glanced at Stephanie Gamp. "I'm feeling sleepy," he said in the anxious tones of someone who confesses to travel sickness. "What can I do?"

"Count something," Lady Gamp suggested.

"Like what?"

She felt like saying, "Sheep," but didn't. The Grey Man was misled, not intrinsically evil. "Trees," she said. "See how many of them you can spot before we get there."

The Grey Man looked out of the window. After a while he said, "One. . ."

The idea of counting sheep stuck with Lady Gamp. Would it be such a bad thing if the Monorath was to take a nap? His absence from the scene (she couldn't bring herself to say 'his death') would be a solution. Bess was almost fond of the brute, but she was only a girl, a sentimental child. Lady Gamp knew the Monorath was merely pacified, not reformed, by their calming influence. He was a monster whose instinct was destruction.

She bent her head down to where he lay. "Sleep," she murmured. "Sleep. . ."

The Monorath heard the voice he quite liked, speaking soothingly. He began to think pleasant thoughts, like what he would like to do to the Destructor one day . . . He thought of something new and unspeakably horrid and grunted.

Lady Gamp felt her feet rise up as the beast beneath her started to grow. "Stop it!" she said sharply, and gave up the idea.

The Monorath subsided and Lady Gamp too gazed out of the window and began to look for trees.

In the Skyhawk Grandpa Blake was the map reader. He also monitored the instrument panel, since Travis flew by instinct alone. Outside the little cabin the dark air rushed by unevenly, tearing at patches of wispy cloud, but on the instrument panel the artificial horizon was steady, showing that the Cessna was flying dead level.

"Piece of cake, this," Travis remarked complacently.

Bess leaned forward. "But what do we do when we get there?" she asked. "Are we going to be there before them?"

Tom cut in, "We warn this publisher man – right?"

Travis became less cocky at once. "Ah, well . . . no. I mean to say, what would we tell him? A creature out of a book is about to arrive and shred you like a bundle of rags?"

"We see them off, don't we?" Grandpa suggested. "The, um, the people we want to prevent from doing whatever it is they want to do. Something unspeakable, isn't it? Well, we can't have that, so we send them packing."

"Precisely. That, in a nutshell, is the plan." Travis beamed. "We intercept them. I can quite see why the Creator enjoyed your company, Arthur. Invaluable type to have around! The question is: Are we ahead of them?"

They were not. The convoy had left the M40 and was motoring at great speed down country lanes near Wychwood Forest. In the estate car Mr Jackson saw the old Rolls-Royce come to a skidding stop by a faded signpost, slewing into the grass verge.

"He slammed the handbrake on. Should have changed down in one smooth motion and braked using a regular pressure of the foot," he remarked to Marbles, putting his words into action. He had enjoyed his spell at the wheel.

"What is it? Are we lost?"

"Oh, yes. I expect so."

Despite his excellent driving they too had come very sharply to a halt. Mr Jackson asked, "Everyone all right in the back?"

"I think we're one short," came a voice from the pile of Grey Men behind him.

"Yes, we are," another said. "Someone nodded off around Warwick."

Cap came running from the Rolls-Royce. He had been overexcited ever since he used the magic credit card at the service station half an hour ago.

"Get out! Get out!"

"Why? D'you need a push?" Marbles enquired.

"Don't be foolish. We're there! I don't know how Gloria did it but she got us straight there. See?" He waved at the signpost. "Adcock House. We'll do the rest on foot – quieter. Lots of trees for cover. . ."

"Surprise him, you mean," Mr Jackson said cheerfully. "And how!"

Gordon Haines was not a man who was surprised by much. He had risen to a position of eminence in the publishing profession by making sure that if there was any surprising to be done, he would be the one to do it. He was a plump and vastly competent bachelor of fifty, with a shiny bald head and an equally polished way of life.

Adcock House was one of the more unimaginative Regency villas one comes across, with the clean lines of a big white shoebox. Over the years it had become a superior executive residence, with unobtrusive solar heating and statues of some value littering the rolling lawn. These necessities had been purchased by dint of ferocious hard work and the wee small hours found Gordon crouched over a warm computer in the first-floor library, his glistening head reflecting the white light from the discreet halogen light fittings in the moulded ceiling. His modem was connected and someone in Australia was shortly about to get a red-hot fax. His fingers fairly raced over the keyboard.

NO MORE EXCUSES, SCOTT. Your client undertook to provide me with the text and pictures of an attractive book on royalty and their taste in snack foods. Our contract clearly provides for a chapter on what royalty eat in bed, along with photographs, preferably of a suggestive nature. To date no such chapter or picture has been forthcoming. Hasn't the man heard of telephoto camera lenses? I hate Tasty Tips from the Very Top as a title and if the aforementioned chapter does not reach me soon your client will be in breach of contract and will incur a substantial financial penalty.

Gordon was going on to explain that while he, personally, had no interest in royalty, nor their methods of preparing foodstuffs in microwave ovens, Germany and France *had*, when he heard the noise of breaking glass somewhere in the house.

Already pumped up with righteous rage, he was infuriated by the interruption.

Instead of phoning the police, he snatched up an antique silver paperknife and tiptoed daintily and very fast to the panelled door. With a swift movement he flung it wide and was face to face with the towering figure of Marbles.

"Good evening, sunshine."

Marbles had no means of knowing that a publisher working on an international deal is not a man to be trifled with. Without wasting words, Gordon jabbed him with the paperknife. The silver tool bent double and Marbles chucked Gordon some distance across the room, where he landed on a Regency side table and reduced it to Regency kindling.

"You want to be careful, Sunshine," Marbles admonished him. "You could hurt someone with a dagger like that."

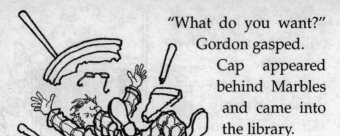

"What do you want?" Gordon gasped.

Cap appeared behind Marbles and came into the library.

"What we want, Mr Haines, is that you re-issue every Fortrain book ever written and commission another one."

"You must be mad!" Gordon blurted out, after doing some very quick mental arithmetic. He reckoned his company stood to lose £276,000 if he included the cost of the side table.

"Oh, no. I'm not mad." Cap smiled the reckless smile. "But I've got something out here that is. . ."

Chapter

8

In the Skyhawk Tom was discovering the disadvantages of air travel. In the first place, if the engine is misbehaving it is not quite as simple as steering a car out of traffic; secondly, if you want to go on living, your machine must come down on a long and relatively flat tract of ground. If time is a factor you hope such an area can be found close to your destination.

The engine was beginning to sound like an industrial-strength tumble dryer filled with a load of sand and pebbles and the occasional broken bottle. Even Travis was worried and Grandpa, with his knowledge of flying and its perils, was plain scared. They had found Wychwood Forest, the major landmark near Adcock House, but after circling several times in the dark still had no idea where the publisher's dwelling was located.

Sweat ran into Grandpa's eyes, though it was cold up there. "Leave it! Just keep going – if you can – till you see somewhere to put her down. I should have serviced her . . . I must be crazy to have even thought of this!"

There was a note of irritation in Travis's response. "There's no point at all in landing twenty miles from where we need to be. Do that and it would have been quicker to make the whole journey by horse and cart."

"There's nowhere suitable here! Too many trees!"

"I shall use the force of my not inconsid-

144

erable imagination to keep us airborne, should all else fail," Travis said loftily. "But I refuse to abandon Plan A until it is forced upon me."

Bess said to Tom, "If we crash, I'll do what I can for you."

Tom found a desperate kind of humour. "Would that be before or after I'm dead?"

In the library, Gordon Haines was over his initial shock. His portliness and the collapsing table had cushioned his fall and it was his pride that hurt most. Cap had described himself as the leader of an action group which would not take no for an answer, but they had almost immediately become bogged down in a dispute about the merits of the Fortrain books. Gloria took it all very personally.

"What about the bit in *The Great Plain* when Princess Gloriana speaks to her people about how she feels about the coming war? Now that is a great speech".

"Derivative," Gordon sneered. "Elizabeth the First said it much better at Tilbury."

Cap said, "Listen, you don't get it. We don't care what you think about the books, you're going to throw your weight behind them again. I told you, we don't take no for an answer!"

Gordon said icily, "All right, then, this is not an answer, it is my *decision*. And the word is still no."

Cap flashed his teeth. "An adversary worthy of my steel, I see. Time for trouble, my little sunbeam. Let's try it the easy way first. Dust him down, Mr Jackson, and hold him tight."

Mr Jackson did so and Gloria advanced, wriggling her hips so much it looked as if she had a bad leg. "Honey, I can handle this." She put her hand behind her neck to plump up her hair. "Mr Haines – or can I call you Sweetie? Be a nice publisher and you and I can spend a little time together! How about it, Sugar-lump?"

"That is a grotesque idea, madam."

Des appeared from behind Marbles. "I think I know how to get to him," he said in his reverberating voice. He lowered the mighty organ to a menacing growl. "Now listen good, Haines. Do what we want, or. . ."

"Or what?"

"Or . . . else."

"Good try, Des," Cap said wearily. He pulled the leather-clad Destructor aside and pushed his face into the publisher's. "Does the word 'hypnotism' mean anything to you?"

"Writers have frequently attempted to hypnotise me. None succeeded."

Cap widened his eyes and threw back his head, letting his eyes blaze down on Haines.

Who said interestedly, "I can see right up your nose when you do that."

Cap only smiled. Gordon had begun to feel he was getting the upper hand in all this, but this slow smile alarmed him.

Cap said with feigned helplessness, "Well, no one can say we didn't try. Go and stir up the Monorath a little, will you, Des?"

The Skyhawk laboured up into the sky. Travis wanted to make one last sweep, and the last time around they had gone so low they had nearly crashed into a copse of trees.

Grandpa and Tom were silent. Tom was scared and felt guilty because he was somehow responsible for putting Grandpa's life in danger. He wanted to apologise, but his mouth was dry and his tongue seemed numb.

There was a diminutive klaxon sound and Grandpa came to life.

"Stall warning! Get the nose down!"

"Mmn," was all Travis said and he continued the climb, slowing all the while, until it seemed the plane would come to a standstill in the sky. He was at last levelling off with what he inwardly thought of as "a sure yet delicate touch", when the engine cut out completely. The aeroplane immediately tried to point its nose earthwards and Travis allowed it a shallow dive until the controls could steady it. Along with the wind they could hear the structural creaks and squeaks of the flying machine, which had been transformed into a very heavy glider.

Unflustered, Travis said quietly, "Well,

we didn't make it. They got there first."

"What?" Bess asked.

"Saw it a moment ago – there on the port side. At last! Let me trim this thing. . ." He worked the flaps and the rudder again and the Skyhawk wobbled sideways, dipping a wing and turning. They could all see a small, faint glow about a kilometre away.

"Wasn't there before, was it?"

"No," Grandpa said tightly. "Now get us down!"

"Well, of course." And Travis put the plane into a much steeper dive, aiming it directly at what he believed must be Adcock House. He said conversationally, "I'm going to bring up the nose short of the target and stall us on purpose. Which will be tricky."

"We'll drop like a stone," Grandpa whispered.

On the lawn were two tall pine trees set quite close together. Des was hiding behind one of them, having put some distance between himself and the Monorath. His close proximity had had the desired effect: the beast had swollen to twice his previous size and in his overexcitement had become much more than simply glowing, taking on the heating properties of a furnace. Until Des had left the room, Cap had not been able to direct the Monorath to Gordon Haines.

Elsewhere on the big lawn the Grey Men stood with the statues, so that together they looked like a gathering under a palace window, waiting perhaps for news of a royal birth. Two of them held Lady Gamp captive. The whole scene was illumined by the unearthly light emanating from the library, which also gave forth belching growls as the Monorath worked himself into a state.

"This is wrong!" Stephanie Gamp cried melodramatically, trying to wrench herself free. "We didn't come here for this kind of thing!" Then she added less forcefully, because she was genuinely surprised, "Look out behind! There's an aeroplane coming towards us!" She bellowed to the Grey Men and Des, "Get out of the way! Look behind you!

Tom was leaning forward between Grandpa and Travis as they swept down towards the house. On the lawn some figures ran from the oncoming plane and others stayed curiously still. With four hundred metres to go, Travis dipped a wing, aligning the plane so that it was pointing at the small space between the two high pine trees. A man in leather was running away from the trees as fast as his short legs could carry him. The motionless figures were statues, Tom realised.

"We're going in too steep! This is it!" Grandpa shouted. "It's been a good life!"

Travis levelled the Skyhawk, corrected for drift and dropped the elephantine Fowler flaps. The aeroplane heaved up its nose and stalled and then swept down again steeply. Travis fought to wrench up the nose one last time and they were almost skimming the ground, racing towards the gap between the pines. With an instinct for doom, Tom saw that they were travelling much too fast and the space between the trees was too small.

The Skyhawk touched down, bounced up and rushed between the trees, which ripped the broad wings off, along with the cabin roof.

The wheels collapsed and the fuselage tobogganed on, slowing all the time. In the shattered cabin Travis grabbed Grandpa and Bess held on tightly to Tom. The remnants of the plane came to a sickeningly abrupt halt against a naked woman who was failing to cover herself with what might have been a bath towel. Being solid marble, she did not protest but toppled face first into the lawn. They were ten metres from the paved terrace of Adcock House, where the Grey Men and Des had gathered.

"Brilliantly judged," Travis congratulated himself. He unstrapped himself and stood up to wave to Lady Gamp. "Stephanie, darling!"

"Travesty – that was magnificent!" she called back, still pinioned by two Grey Men.

"It was extremely dangerous. Get out, quick!" Grandpa urged and added to Travis, "You wrecker!"

As they clambered out, he continued, "But it was a tremendous feat – don't get me wrong."

Bess murmured to Tom, "Out of the frying pan into the fire."

Taking on the burden of command, Des had indicated to the Grey Men to surround the plane.

One of them asked neutrally, "I suppose it's a limb-from-limb job, is it?"

"Oh, go ahead," Travis said contemptuously. "While you still have the strength. But if you do, I very much doubt you'll ever see Fortrain again – not with Captain Magnificent calling the shots."

No one moved or said anything. Light pulsed in the library above them and the Monorath howled terribly. Des shivered and all at once looked uncertain.

Seeing this, Tom felt a spurt of confidence. He said boldly, "Well, come on, then! If you're in charge here, what are you going to do?"

"I know what to do – don't worry about that!"

"Well, let's see it," Travis chivvied him. "Do it!"

Des struggled frantically for an idea and then something in him snapped. "Oh, leave me alone, will you? What's the point? It's all so hopeless here." His voice thickened with emotion. "No one takes the blindest bit of notice of me. I'm threatened by a creature who's supposed to look up to me. And . . . and I feel exhausted."

It was a premonition of death that fretted the Grey Men. One of them said dejectedly, "We're all tired. In the books I got to be different people and do exciting things. It's ghastly here – quite unreal! People go shopping and watch television!"

Des's mouth twisted down like a baby's and his bottom lip trembled. "It's not even as though Cap's getting us anywhere. I was up there. That publisher is a tough nut. All that's going to happen is Cap's going to let the Monorath tear him to pieces. Then where will we be?"

"Let me help you," Travis offered with quiet compassion. "Let me take care of you all. I began the whole thing: let me try and sort it out."

Lady Gamp said briskly, "One step forward, everyone who wants Travesty-Warlock as boss."

"'Travis', Stephanie darling. I'm Travis now."

"Ooh. Attractive," Lady Gamp said coyly.

The sight of the Monorath had knocked all pride out of Gordon Haines. White hot, the creature was now much larger than a pig and, in all-too-vivid close-up, not much like one. Three metres long and nearly two metres high, he had a pale, sagging, naked face with a terrible kind of beak in the centre; flaps of loose flesh hung down obscuring his small red eyes, and his bulbous body was covered in rolls of drooping white skin, so that he looked like an overblown grub. He moved on twenty pink-bottomed suckers, which rucked up the carpet dreadfully as he advanced inexorably towards Gordon Haines in a horrifying dance of entrapment. Both hunter and hunted made the most disgusting noises of blood-lust or fear, and their rapt audience had completely failed to register that outside a plane had crash-landed.

At last the remnants of his nerve failed him and Gordon dived beneath his desk with a despairing squeak, making himself into what he hoped was an impregnable stone-shape. The dark space was so confined there was barely room to tremble.

Now the Monorath's monstrous beak foraged around Gordon's rear quarters

and tugged off one of his shoes. They both howled.

"Publish and be saved!" came Cap's voice.

"This isn't happening! I'm having a breakdown!"

"You stubborn old goat! Are you going to issue a contract?"

"There wouldn't be any point! C. M. Furnival is a desperately sick man – he may even be dying!"

"Rubbish! Cunning – typically cunning – but simple deceit can't save you now! The end is nigh, Mr Haines. Agree to my terms or after a count of five the Monorath will scatter pieces of you all over the room!"

Gordon squeezed himself even smaller. "He's not real! Do what you like! This is awful!" He began to whimper uncontrollably.

"I'm going to start counting. Five . . . Oh, forget it. Zero. Bend him! Rend him! Do your worst, Great Beast!"

The Monorath howled with pleasure and raised his terrible beak with terrible force, overturning the heavy desk as if it were cardboard. Then, at an unearthly speed, he grew upwards into the shape of a great fat snake until his head hit the high ceiling. His beak grew yet larger and opened wide. The publisher had rolled over and looked up it. In the ghastly bone mouth were a thousand black wriggling tongues. The head went back, tensing to strike. . .

The library doors burst open and a palace revolution swept into the room, headed by Travis in his linen suit. Caught up in the fervour of it all, Tom was at his elbow.

"Nobody move!" Travis commanded. "This is a takeover." To the Monorath he said, "Stay!"

The Monorath held his threatening position but there was doubt in his little eyes.

Gloria and Marbles had at once looked to Cap for instruction. Mr Jackson only raised his eyebrows, twitched up the trousers on his hairy suit and sat down on a plush chaise longue to observe developments. It was clear to all that, with the

Grey Men on their side, the rebels were in the majority.

"What does this mean?" Cap said with a ruler's hauteur.

From where she stood at Grandpa's side, Lady Gamp forced her way through the crowd and said, "It means an end to your rule, Cap. An end to vanity and self-will run riot. Travis is our leader now."

Travis asked incisively, "Where's Mr Haines? Has the Monorath already done his worst? Developing an uncontrollable blood-lust in the process?"

Mr Jackson spoke up. "He's that thing on the floor. Gone a bit quiet, though."

Travis walked boldly past the Monorath's great bulk and investigated. "Seems to be in some kind of coma."

Cap was livid, in the grip of an icy rage. "Will everyone stop taking his lead? I am the commander. We do what I say!"

"Not any more, Cap," Travis answered. "You're outnumbered and outvoted."

Captain Magnificent's eyes shot sparks of hatred. "I should have known it would come to this, Travesty-Warlock! A challenge from some bit-part player!"

"No, Cap. We are brothers, you and I, each representing a part of the Creator's being. Your successes in the books have gone to your head: my reverses have kept me humble."

"Not humble enough by far. I'll make you humble!" Cap swaggered over to Travis with athletic arrogance. "Nobody do a thing! This is between me and the old man."

He began to focus his eyes on the wizard's.

Chapter

9

Travis did not flinch from Cap's burning stare. Instead he took a step towards him. The others in the room were transfixed by the deadly confrontation, while from high above them the Monorath's little red eyes looked down sideways at the action.

Cap said softly, "Did nobody ever tell you the rules, old man? The hero always survives. His helpers are expendable."

Travis frowned, resisting the power of Cap's stare. He said nothing. Cap's eyes began to blaze and everyone in the room saw a shimmy of power failure run through Travis.

"Change, Travis!" Tom shouted. "Be magic!"

Travis did not look away from Cap, saying only, "Can't waste the energy, Tom."

Cap began, for the first time, to glow with the energy he was putting forth. With an enormous effort Travis lifted up his head and stared him full in the eye. Cap was going white-hot; the room became sweltering and a luminous haze surrounded him. The two creations kept their gazes locked.

Then, at what must have been quite literally the speed of light, Cap disappeared. He had burned himself out.

Gloria screamed, "No! *Nooooo!*"

Where Cap had stood, a thin vapour subsided to the carpet. Travis said quickly, "Marbles, Mr Jackson – here. And you Stephanie. And Bess. You too, Gloria."

Numbly they came to him. "He's not quite gone. Look at where he was and think of him – hard," Travis said and began to concentrate his own powers anew.

The stifling heat grew and grew. Tom looked at the spreading mist where Cap had been and thought of him. The magnificent Prince Bramnoc, lost for ever. It couldn't be true.

And then the mist swirled together and Cap was back as suddenly as he had vanished, lying quite still on the rucked carpet under the combined stares of his peers.

Travis went and knelt by him, lifting the handsome, lolling head. "My dear fellow," he said with trembling sincerity. "My dear old fellow."

Cap's eyes opened. He murmured, "Hello, Travesty. What happened? Don't tell me I lost."

"Nobody lost. Not now you're back. What happened was that you forgot something you used to know, that's all: to be a hero, you have to be heroic."

"Don't follow you. . ." Cap was still groggy.

"It doesn't matter. Tell you later."

Cap looked at him and smiled. It was

not like the old, cruel smile. He said tranquilly, "OK. You're the boss. What happens now?"

Gloria rushed to him and Travis got to his feet. "Could someone be kind to the Monorath? He needs a *lot* of petting and stroking. And we must revive our publisher. Marbles, pick him up – gently."

Bess went to the Monorath and began stroking while Travis strode back to the overturned desk. Amazingly, the computer and modem and telephone were still working where they lay on the floor, all three of them beeping faintly as though echoing Gordon's distressed state. Travis frowned, bent down and pressed a lot of keys hopefully. The computer screen had gone dead, so he was unaware that he had erased Gordon's current document and brought up another, shorter letter he had intended to send elsewhere, to someone very dear to him. In dumb obedience to Travis's random fingering, a fax winged its way to the Australian literary agent. 'YOU'RE MY LITTLE TOOT-SIE AND I LOVE YOU.' Then the machines fell silent and Travis turned to face the others.

"He's all limp," Marbles said of the publisher he dangled from one large hand. "Alive, though."

Some minutes later the Monorath had shrunk by a quarter and others in the room were calmer too. Cap had taken over the chaise longue, with Gloria cradling his head in her lap. He was pale yet serene; almost, one might say, a shadow of the man he had been.

Another in the room was also not himself. Gordon Haines had at last opened his eyes but had been found to be in a state of shock so deep he could not be reached. He sat on his rucked carpet looking wan and occasionally coming out with pithy yet unintelligible comments.

"Microwave Majesty," he said.

Meanwhile the library was being wrecked even more. With Gordon unable to talk, Travis had ordered a search of his records to find out where the Creator was. Whole shelves were being pulled from the walls and Marbles had taken it upon himself to further dismantle the desk.

Leafing through various files their

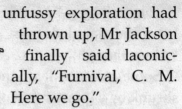

unfussy exploration had thrown up, Mr Jackson finally said laconically, "Furnival, C. M. Here we go."

He held up a cardboard folder for their new leader to see. Travis took it and sat in Gordon's chair to go through it. In the folder were various letters and documents and some pages of orderly notes.

They all gathered around to await Travis's reaction. He frowned as he read and they could see rapidly changing emotions course across his face.

"What is it?" Bess asked. "What's in there?"

As fast as his eyes could traverse the paper, Travis read more of the notes. "Well . . ." he said slowly. "Well. There's some very, very good news . . . and some very, very bad news."

"Yes?" said Bess.

"The good news is that the Creator isn't too far from here. He's not abroad any more. He's living somewhere where Mr Haines can go and visit him quite easily – and not so far from the Manor either, if I guess right."

"So what's the bad news?" Mr Jackson asked.

"He's in a nursing home. He has become feeble-minded and can't look after himself."

It was a bombshell.

"That's why he was flown home from Italy. Our chum Mr Haines arranged it. It would appear that he is, in his hard-headed way, a good friend. He even managed to keep it out of the papers. Which from our point of view was not helpful. The doctors don't know what's wrong with the Creator. He won't talk and he seems to have lost the will to live."

Marbles joked heavily, "Perhaps he misses us."

Travis sprang to his feet. "Yes – yes! That's *it*! Marbles, thank you!"

Confused, the big man said, "Oh, that's all right."

"Don't you see it? We are portions of his personality – with so many of us out of him, he's empty. He has no energy without us."

Unexpectedly, one of the Grey Men put his oar in. "*We* haven't got much energy without *him*. Not any more."

He was having severe identity problems, flickering like neon when you first switch it on, and a couple of the others did not look too hot either. The tumultuous night had taken its toll on their stamina. But for some of the characters, the excitement had strengthened their individuality and hold on life. Mr Jackson said brightly, "Oh, I don't know. I feel better than ever."

Travis shot him a glance. "I'm very happy for you. But we have to face it: our time here is up. If any of us ever wish to see Fortrain again, we must help the Creator pull through – and there's no time to be lost."

"You mean. . .?" Des prompted tremulously.

"Yes. We're going home."

A soft bubbling sigh came from somewhere in the room.

Tom said, "Look at the Monorath!"

Travis whirled round, but his apprehension was unfounded. The Monorath was cooling and shrinking at a vastly increased rate.

"How did that happen?" Gloria asked shrilly. "Who did that?"

Bess knew. As he shrank, his head nearing hers by the second, she whispered to the ugly beast, "Home. You're going home."

Travis addressed the rest of them. "We'll have to get back to the Manor at some point. I'm not leaving anyone behind."

The Monorath squidged himself towards Travis gratefully. The monster was pig-size again and the folds of flesh were looser than before. Tom wondered just how big he could get if he wanted to. Big enough to fill all that elastic drapery of skin?

Travis said to him, "You've been upset.

It's not good for you. But don't worry – there'll be little more of this world for you to put up with. I've got a special conveyance for you!"

The Monorath put his grotesque head on one side enquiringly, and Travis smiled. "You're going to travel in young Tom."

There was a blank silence and then, somehow, Tom was able to convey in three words a whole range of negative emotions concerning this scheme.

"Oh, no – *look*. . .!"

Travis, however, had never been happier. "Oh, come now – what better repository could he have? The world of the mind is, after all, the beast's natural habitat and what could be more perfect than the mind of a young boy? A young boy with a vivid imagination, familiar with the books . . . where could he possibly feel more at home?"

"But what about me? How will *I* feel?"

Travis looked hurt. "I hope you're not going to get sulky about a perfectly straightforward act of selflessness. I'm disappointed in you, young Tom."

"Travis." It was Bess and she was not

looking at Travis with any great affection.

"Yes, young Bess?"

"Would you like to be honest with Tom and tell him that, all along, this was your plan for him?"

"Well, no . . . I wouldn't *like* to . . . but it is, of course, true."

A Grey Man had a sensational thought and put his hand up. "Hey, could I travel in him too?"

Several other Grey Men at once began raising their hands and clamouring to share the privilege, but Travis quelled the lot of them with an uncharacteristic loss of temper.

"Be silent! Foolish jackals! Do you think I would do anything to endanger the well-being of my young friend? The Monorath will be quite enough company for him, thank you very much! I'm sorry, but you all chose to come here and you must fend for yourselves! Now. Tom. Come here."

Drearily, Tom did as he was told. He was tired and fearful.

Travis said very gently, "It's your decision. Will you do it?"

"I suppose I'll have to, won't I?"

"We're all very grateful. We really couldn't take any more chances with what is, after all, a monster . . . Look at me, Tom. Do you trust me?"

His eyes were beseeching . . . deep and beseeching. If you looked far enough into them, you knew you could trust him. "Yes," said Tom faintly.

Travis whispered, "Good," and kept staring at him, and then there was nothing at all.

When there was something again, it was rapid motion. Waking from a dreamless sleep, Tom heard the licking, holding sound of big car tyres eating up the road. His eyelids were still stuck together by tiredness. When they popped apart he saw a red leather seat in front of him, containing Travis, who was driving the Rolls-Royce. Beside him sat Mr Jackson and with him, crammed into the large seat, was someone even smaller: Bess.

Tom looked to his right. Gordon Haines was crushed up against him, looking sombre. His eyes met Tom's.

"Royal Jellies," the publisher said quietly. Embarrassed, Tom looked to his left.

Cap was slumped against Lady Gamp, staring into space. Lady Gamp was in her motherly mode, nursing him and stroking his hair. Tom noticed that his skin looked suspiciously translucent.

Lady Gamp explained Gordon's presence. "We have to keep him with us. He could be a danger to us when he snaps out of it, and until he does he needs looking after."

"Is Cap all right?" Tom asked.

"No. And we've lost some more of the Grey Ones. We've outstayed our welcome here – that's what it is."

Travis glanced in the rear-view mirror. "Too much excitement. And more to come, I'm afraid."

Bess turned round in her seat and asked brightly, "So how are you getting on with your new friend?"

"New friend?"

"The Monorath. Travis got him into you. Is it OK?"

"Yes, I think so." Tom sat up straighter, shocked. He tried to analyse how he felt. So far he was no different from before, as far as he could tell, except that he was so tired . . . but then, he'd been awake most of the night and had eaten nothing.

"Where's Grandpa?" he asked, trying to sound normal.

"He took the other car to Marshton Manor," Travis said. "He picks up the stragglers and we all meet at the nursing home. That's the plan, anyway."

"He's got Gloria and Des and a bunch of the Grey Ones," said Bess with enjoyment. "It must be ghastly. Gloria won't stop being dramatic about Cap. She'd have bored him to sleep the way she was carrying on."

"It's not that I want to publish all these royalty books," Gordon announced. "It's just the way things have gone." He added cunningly, "Throne-Room Delicacies. Yum yum."

"I'm awfully hungry," Tom discovered.

Mr Jackson said to Travis, "We need more petrol too – we'll have to stop somewhere. This old bus is thirstier than a steelworker on Chilli Chips."

Travis spoke loudly. "Cap? How are you doing? Can you work the credit card for us?"

With a huge effort, Cap lifted his head from Lady Gamp's shoulder. "I'll try," he said almost inaudibly. Twenty minutes later the Rolls-Royce pulled into a service station on the motorway. The sky was losing its purple dye, bleaching itself in preparation for the morning.

The service station had a small café attached and some long-distance lorry drivers were in it, eating hugely. Travis eased the big old car to a stop and got out. He came round to open the door for Lady Gamp and between them they helped Cap out. He still cut a magnificent figure; if anything, his exhaustion added to his noble bearing.

Travis said to Mr Jackson, "Keep an eye on our Gordon. Oh, Tom – could you get any cash out of him? It'd be easier. You must be hungry."

"I'll try," said Tom.

Lady Gamp helped Cap out of the car and stood with him under the glaring yellow sodium lights of the service station while Travis started to unscrew the cap on the tank of the Rolls-Royce.

Tom turned to Gordon Haines, sitting beside him. "Um, excuse me . . . could you lend me some money?"

Gordon regarded him sternly. "You want an advance?"

"Um, yes."

"No," the publisher said with satisfaction.

"Well, I could write you something – about royalty and . . . um. . ." He was stuck.

Gordon reached for his wallet. "Palace lavatories of the world. There's five pounds. Don't spend it all on drink."

Feeling guilty, Tom took the note and got out of the car. Bess came with him, compelled by her curiosity about food. In the café none of the men sitting there took any notice of them. Watched enviously by Bess, Tom bought sandwiches and a soft drink. The girl behind the till was dumb with tedium and said nothing as she handed him his change, but then, looking past them vacantly, her eyes widened in astonishment.

Tom looked round. Standing by the window where you paid for petrol, one of the creations was on the blink, losing and regaining substance in flashing waves. It was not Cap, but Lady Gamp. . .

Poker-faced, Tom looked back at the girl behind the till.

"Did you see that?" she gasped.

"What?"

Bess had seen too. Coolly she said to the girl, "You don't look well at all. I think you've got a temperature. You should lie down." They hurried from the café.

Cap was signing the credit slip slowly. Meanwhile Travis had opened the boot of the car. Inside it, Marbles sat up.

"Sorry, Travis. They didn't make it." There had been three Grey Men in there with him when they set out.

"This is getting worse and worse. Look after Cap for a second, will you?"

Marbles went over to him while Travis led Lady Gamp back to the Rolls-Royce, with his arm around her waist, tenderly.

Bess said, "We've got to get on – and quickly."

The man behind the payment window, who had seen nothing, returned the credit card to Cap. "You're someone famous, aren't you? Haven't I seen you on the telly?"

Cap smiled wanly and his handsome face came to life. He murmured, "Star quality. You can't hide it."

Marbles supported him on the walk back to the Rolls-Royce, moving fast, so that Cap's feet barely touched the ground. Travis had put Lady Gamp in already and was starting the engine.

The man at the payment window watched the activity with curiosity. He thought the bustle was because Cap was someone famous who was worried about having been recognised. The guy with the long white hair was obviously his manager. Hello, what was happening now? The really huge guy was the bodyguard, presumably. Where had he come from? Now he was . . . he was getting into the boot of the Rolls-Royce.

The two cars squealed out of the service station and the man sighed. Back to the real world. . .

In the car Travis kept looking in the mirror at Lady Gamp. "Are you all right now, Steph?" he asked with loving anxiety.

"No, I'm still coming and going . . . I'm sorry, Travesty."

"Nothing to be sorry about. You're going to make it. I promise." He looked back at the road and pressed hard on the accelerator. "I wonder how they're doing in the other car."

Sounding frightened, Lady Gamp quoted Shakespeare. "'We are such stuff as dreams are made on . . . And . . . and our little life is rounded with a sleep. . .'"

"Stay awake, Steph. It's the mother in

you – you've been giving your energy to Cap. Talk, move about, anything – but *don't* go to sleep."

With Cap lolling across her, Lady Gamp fought to sit up straighter. With a ghastly cheerfulness she said, "I must say, with my connexion to Dickens, I thought I would have been made of sterner stuff." She sought Tom's attention. "It's true, you know, I am descended from Sairah Gamp – in the direct line. I have always been proud of my association with Mr Dickens – poor man! A febrile mind, eventually quite consumed by character."

Eating a cheese sandwich, Tom was feeling drowsy. Mother Gamp had always bored him with her monologues. She went on, with forced brightness, to discuss how Dickens himself had always had a special affection for *Martin Chuzzlewit* and how *she* had always regarded it as his comic masterpiece . . . Tom's eyes closed and the cheese sandwich released itself from his grasp and fell to the floor.

The Rolls-Royce spend onwards into the dawn and Tom slept again. And dreamed.

Chapter

The Monorath was sitting in the back of a mathematics class in Tom's school, which here was whiter, brighter and bigger than in reality. The class was bored, but the Monorath was enjoying himself. It was clear the young people had no more idea of what the teacher was talking about than he, the Monorath, had. For the first time in his existence he felt included; he felt he was a part of something.

"Compound fractions," the teacher said impatiently. "Come on, you lot. We were talking about them yesterday. Or, at least, I was . . . Someone? Anyone?"

The Monorath swelled with pride. He knew the answer to this one. Like any other schoolboy, however, he did not want to set himself apart from the group by exhibiting knowledge, so stayed smugly silent.

"Why do I bother?" the teacher declaimed. "I'm warning you – it'll be a detention for every man-jack of you!"

A rustle of discontent went round the class. The Monorath was discontented too. He had no idea what a detention was, but it was unpopular with his new friends and that was enough for him.

"Someone must know *something* about compound fractions," the teacher said despairingly.

The Monorath suckered himself forwards and rose up, revealing his pale belly. It was as if he was raising his hand. He did know something about the subject under discussion. In fact, there wasn't much you could teach him about compound fractures. You snaffled some limb – an arm, or it might be a leg – in your beak, and then you wrenched it as you bit into it and . . . Unable to speak, he moaned and acted out the requisite actions. Heads turned, among them Tom's, and the Monorath's moans were drowned in a general scream. The teacher led the flight from the classroom.

The Monorath stayed behind and sulked. There was no pleasing some people. You helped them out and they all dashed off to have fun somewhere else, without you. Absently he toured the classroom, wrecking it. But it was dull with no one to watch his feats of destruction. Finally he ripped the door off a large cupboard and saw a gaping black space beyond. He was unsurprised, since the world of the imagination was his natural environment. He made himself smaller and squirmed into the space, which opened out immediately.

Though he did not know it, he was in a

version of Tom's bedroom – the one he would never see again, in the house they were moving from. Here it was represented as a dusty, cavernous room such as a church hall. It was quite empty except for the small bed about thirty metres away, up against the wall. It was dark and gloomy here and the Monorath cheered up, feeling at home. There was rather a jolly atmosphere of fear.

A shape in the bed sat up suddenly. It was Tom. He leaned down as though to look under the bed but panicked and retreated under his duvet, hiding himself entirely.

The Monorath narrowed his red eyes. There was a specific cause for this feeling of terror – and it wasn't him. There was some other horror hiding under the bed!

All his life the Monorath had thought of himself as 'the one and only'. The idea of competition of any kind was abhorrent to him. He roared with rage and defiance and began to grow. By the time he had finished growing, the giant suckers that were his legs had no distance at all to travel to the bed.

In the Rolls-Royce Tom shouted and thrashed about, contributing greatly to Lady Gamp's fight for wakefulness.

"Writers!" Gordon Haines said with contempt. "No self-discipline – not one of them!"

"Should we wake him up?" Travis asked Lady Gamp.

Tom rose to the surface from his deep dream and opened his eyes, unaware of the commotion he had caused. "Wow!" he said, expelling all the tension from his body on one long, shaky breath.

"Are you all right?" Bess asked, seriously worried for him.

"Yes.

It was a dream. That's all."

"What happened?"

"I don't know. I wasn't looking. It's OK – it's over now."

"Truly?"

"Yes, really. I feel fine."

And he did.

"Look!" Bess squealed.

"What?"

"A horse – a real horse! I saw a horse

in that field!"

"Oh, is that all?"

"*Royal Riders*? Coffee-table book?" Gordon suggested.

The early-morning sky was grey and dirty and only a high wind kept off the rain that must some time fall. The Rolls eased its way along the last metres to its destination.

The Branwell Nursing Home was nineteenth-century Gothic, built to threaten. Set in quiet country surroundings, it resembled a retirement home for bats: ivy-clad and complete with tower and crumbling slate roof. It looked its worst in the prevailing weather.

It also looked unassailable. There was a tall fence running all the way round the extensive grounds, with a neat arrangement of barbed wire along the top. Clearly it was hard to get out of and, equally clearly, it would not be easy to get in. Travis brought the car to a standstill outside the big iron gates and contemplated the problem.

"What I would like to do is to walk in

and tell them I'm here to save the life of C. M. Furnival, but I don't think that'd get us very far."

"A diversion. That's what you need," Cap said hoarsely. "Set fire to the place – that kind of thing."

"Feeling a little better, are you? No. That would be to endanger the lives of the inmates, many of whom will be old and frail, and all life must be respected."

Tom said, "Your idea wasn't too bad, actually, Travis. For a start, a Rolls-Royce really impresses people. And you may not have a blue suit, like a doctor, but you look kind of like a professor." Further inspiration came. "And even if he isn't in great shape, we do have Mr Haines with us."

"Can't stay long," the publisher announced importantly. "Got to get to Frankfurt."

Travis turned round to face Tom full on. "Tom Short," he said, "if I had a son I'd like him to be like you. We will take the direct route you propose. Time is the vital factor."

Those in the estate car on the way to Marshton Manor were also concerned about the time element. At the wheel, Grandpa looked into the rear-view mirror. "Hands up who's still here?" he said. "Oh, dear."

There was only one, dangerously indistinct Grey Man left sitting there with Des, who was an unhealthy grey colour himself. The Grey Man said quietly but triumphantly, "One thousand and eighty one. Trees."

Sitting in the front, Gloria had worn out her hysteria about Cap. It was hard to keep up a decent level of hysteria about someone who had lost so much of his *flair*. She said sadly, "I sang to them, but it didn't work."

"Or perhaps it did," Des said meanly. But he looked fearful. "I don't feel good . . . I don't feel good at all."

Gloria was back to her petulant best. "I'm in the wrong car. This one's for has-beens."

The lone Grey Man faded some more and rambled feverishly, "Trees are such lovely things . . . I'm lucky I've seen so many. . ." He smiled to himself and then adjusted his features to look more serious. "You go on without me."

He vanished.

"We're crazy to have separated from the others," Gloria complained. "There's going to be no one left at the Manor anyway."

Grandpa was exhausted and found it hard to concentrate on the road ahead. He tightened his hold on the steering wheel. "Madam, will you please shut it!"

With ease Marbles snapped the rusty padlock on the tall gates and swung them wide for the Rolls-Royce to make its stately progress up the tarmac drive. Travis was excited about the part he had to play and the heavy car rocked as he stopped it rather too quickly.

"Mr Jackson, come with me and take my cues. The rest of you, sit tight."

Tom watched as Travis walked to the front door with Mr Jackson hurrying along by his side. As Travis rang the front doorbell of the lowering institution, Tom had serious doubts about the wisdom of the plan he had suggested. . .

Travis had none. When the door was opened by a trim woman in her thirties, he launched straight into his spiel.

"Madam, good morning. I am aware it is extremely early, but I am here at the urgent behest of Mr Gordon Haines, whom you will see sitting in my motor vehicle. I believe he is known to you?"

Mrs Henrietta Yorke replied coolly, "I do know Mr Haines, but I don't know you. Do you think you could keep your voice down? Our residents are still in bed."

"I take it from your demeanour that you are the Matron here," Travis said, lowering his voice.

"I am the Warden."

"Of course. My colleague – Dr Jackson – and I have been prised from our beds in order that we might assess the health of Mr Furnival, recently arrived here."

"Oh. And you are?"

Travis handed her one of his 'calling cards', with a flourish. "Professor J. M. Travesty-Warlock, PhD. Mr Furnival's case is a matter of interest to me since I am writing a thesis on Lethean turpitude syndrome."

"That may or may not be so, but I should point out that all there is on this piece of paper is your name and nothing else. If indeed it is your name. I have governors to answer to – I can't just let anyone in."

Mr Jackson came into the conflict chirpily. "Look, Miss, um . . ."

"My name is Mrs Yorke, as you should know."

"Yeah – Mrs Yorke. We've been engaged at great expense so's we can – "

"How did you drive in? The gates were locked."

"No, they weren't," Mr Jackson said innocently. "If you've got worries about us, have a quick word with Mr Haines, if you like, though I should warn you he's in a dreadful state about his old mucker."

Mrs Yorke considered. "Very well. Of course I must talk to Mr Haines." Shutting the front door carefully behind her, she led the way to the car. Mr Jackson lingered to try the door surreptitiously. It had locked itself. She must have the keys on her.

Seeing them coming, Tom got out of the Rolls. Marbles was ambling up from the gate in his overalls and Mrs Yorke's mind was not put at rest by their presence.

"Who are those people?" she asked curtly.

The wind was gusting around them so Travis had to lie quite loudly. "My mechanic. And his son. Um, his daughter came too. It's really his day off, but the old car has been playing up recently, so . . . Oh – and I've got my sister with me. See her there? With the slightly mauve hair? And her nephew. He's convalescing after a long illness so he travels everywhere with us."

Mrs Yorke frowned. They had reached the car. "Mr Haines. Good morning. Is it true you wish these gentlemen to see Mr Furnival?"

"Furnival. . ." The name rang a bell with Gordon. "He's not well."

"No, and I'm afraid he's losing his appetite now, too."

"Mmn. Toad in the Hole? Nursery Favourites of the Little Princes?"

"It's a thought, I suppose. . ." Mrs

Yorke was more puzzled by the minute. "But are these men what they say they are?"

Everyone, including Mrs Yorke, waited with interest for his response.

Gordon looked at the Branwell Nursing Home and at Travis. Seeing Cap sitting beside him, with Lady Gamp, he suppressed a little shudder. Things were just beginning to come back to him. He said, "They . . . they have strange powers."

Travis came in with, "While I am a man of science, patients have accredited me with the powers of a healer. Flattering, if it were true."

For the first time he managed to catch her eye full on. He looked deeply and after a second she twitched her head away. "You'd better come in," she said thoughtfully.

Travis and Mr Jackson followed her back to the nursing home. "Did you get to her?" Mr Jackson whispered hopefully.

"No."

Tom watched Mrs Yorke unlock the door and let them in. "I don't like this at all," he said quietly to Bess, who had joined him.

"Why not?" Bess asked. "Seems to be going fine."

"That woman. She looks incredibly practical. Can you do something for me, Bess?"

"Sure. What?"

"You see where the telephone wires go in – there, on the top of the tower?"

"Oh, is that what they are?"

"Yes. I'm not much of a climber. Could you rip them down?"

"Love to," she said and beamed.

She was on her way in a flash. Tom sighed. It might be in a good cause, but the alacrity with which the creations undertook dangerous and illegal activities was unsettling. And catching . . . He said to Marbles, "I think we should get the car turned round, too."

"Cap's not up to it. Shall I give it a go?"

"Oh, all right."

"I was watching Mr Jackson when he did it. I'm a fast learner."

It did not seem likely; still, Marbles's enthusiasm was beyond doubt.

Drivers were about to be changed at Marshton Manor, too. Sleepless, arriving back at an hour when he would normally be getting out of bed, Grandpa was floating beyond any kind of coherent thought, quite unable to rationalise the extraordinary things that had happened and were still happening.

Gloria tripped over to the door in her high heels, rang the bell and yelled, "Anybody home? It's me – Gloria!" She added defiantly, "Lovely as the dawn."

The door was opened almost at once, by the Grey Man who had been on the roof and who had unsuccessfully chased the Skyhawk. He threw his arms around her, crying, "And you are! You are! It's been so long. . .!"

"Back off, fella."

He did so and she saw that he was no longer Grey. He was greyish, it was true, but there was now more than a hint of blue about his suit.

"What came over you?" she asked.

"When the going gets tough, the tough get going. I've been rearranging all the furniture!"

"What's that supposed to mean?"

"They're all gone – every one of them. One by one they took the Big Sleep . . . There's only me left. I did everything I could to stay awake. I sorted the mail, I – "

"We gotta get going. You got a date with the Creator."

She dragged him to the car. Grandpa was asleep. The Grey-Blue Man said, "He doesn't know how lucky he is."

Gloria woke Grandpa up, shaking him roughly. "Snap out of it, Pops! We got some serious driving to do. "

"Can't. Too tired." Grandpa yawned.

"Move over, then, I'll have a go. Or do you want to stay here?"

"Can't. Got to get you there . . . Got to look after young Tom. . ."

She pushed him into the passenger seat. He mumbled, "I'll take over when we're nearly there. I looked at the map . . . it's tricky to get to."

While Gloria attempted a three-point turn, the Grey-Blue Man dashed back to the house for something he had forgotten.

"Harder than it looks, isn't it?" Gloria said happily, producing a sound of mechanical torment from the gearbox.

Travis and Mr Jackson sat waiting on hard armchairs in a small television room with a glass-panelled door. Mrs Yorke had left them here, telling them she would go and see if Mr Furnival was awake.

"Wonder what's on the box," Mr Jackson mused. "I love the telly."

He got up to switch the set on, but Travis stopped him. "Keep your mind on the job in hand. And do something for me. Just check if she's locked the door on us without us knowing."

Mr Jackson stepped lightly to the door. It opened and he looked both ways down the corridor.

He came back, but did not sit down. "Got a bad feeling, Travis. There's two guys with tight white tunics on, loitering both ends of the corridor."

"She *is* a suspicious sort of woman. But there is no reason to believe she won't do as she says she will."

"Your trouble is you think everyone's like you. You're too trusting. Always were, even in the books."

"What do you suggest, then?" Travis asked helplessly.

"They can't hurt us, so we'll give it a few more minutes."

In her office, Henrietta Yorke heard the voice on the telephone say, "Which service do you require?" and answered quietly, "The police."

The line went dead.

Tom was watching Bess. The climb up the ivy had presented no difficulties for her and once at the top of the tower she had not only disengaged the phone wires from their terminals but had very cleverly wrapped them in the ivy so that the lines did not dangle suspiciously. Now she was

climbing down as lightly as a squirrel, undisturbed by the high wind.

Tom was envious. He looked round. Marbles had the Rolls pointing towards the gate: good. He turned to watch Bess again, just as the hairy, snaking strand of ivy she held on to pulled itself away from the wall. She was going to fall. . .

No. She had snatched at new hand-holds and scrambled to a window ledge on the third floor. She grinned down at Tom and then looked in at the window of the room. And looked back at Tom – and beckoned to him frantically.

His heart sank. She beckoned again, with furious passion. He did not have a choice. Feeling sick with nerves, Tom stepped forward and plunged his hands into the ivy, looking for a first hand-hold.

The slightly greasy leaves, the roughness of the clinging plant, the cold gale whipping his hair, all combined to remind him of the natural laws of the world – such as gravity, blood and breaking bones. His hands gripped the ivy with a strength engendered by acute fear and he began to climb.

Chapter

The climb did not get easier. As Tom's arms got tired and his hands began to tremble with the effort, he seemed to double in weight and his fear grew too. The wind seemed stronger and the ivy more slippery the higher he got, though he only looked for the next hand-hold and preferred not to see how far away from the ground he was getting. He had no idea you could feel this frightened outside of a nightmare.

After he had been climbing for what seemed like at least half an hour, swaying on the old ivy and clutching at it desperately, he stopped for a rest.

It was a mistake. Having stopped, he found his momentum had run out. He seized up and was stuck, unable to move at all. He knew if he looked at the ground he would fall and he dared not look up either.

Bess called down from the window ledge, "Come on! Quickly!"

"I can't," Tom whispered.

She could not hear him but his predicament was plain enough. "Don't give up. *Try!* You must."

He squeezed his eyes shut and slowly he reached up a hand and clenched his fist around another stem. In the bleak, blowing darkness he went on up.

Mrs Yorke had summoned the nursing staff to her office. They were her foot soldiers – the kind of characters the Grey Men were required to play in C. M. Furnival's books. Unlike the Grey Men, they were beings of both sexes, in white starched uniforms.

Mrs Yorke addressed them. "I don't like what's going on this morning. The most bizarre people are here and I don't trust them one bit. Sammy, I think the wind may have brought down the telephone line: could you have a look? The rest of you, keep a discreet watch on our visitors both inside and out."

What she lacked in magnetism she made up for in authority and the nurses filed out without asking questions, with the largest of them, Sammy, going to the front door.

Inching up the tower wall, Tom reached out blindly for another hold – and found Bess's hand. The strength of her grip filled him with relief and gratitude and he at last looked up. Bess smiled and helped him to the window ledge she was standing on. Tom ended up kneeling there with his face pressed to the window and shaking all over.

"It's the Creator in there, isn't it?" she asked in a reverent voice.

There was an old man sitting in the middle of the little bedroom, wearing a drab tartan dressing gown. Tom had seen photographs of C. M. Furnival on book covers, but this man was far too old, and so shrunken-looking! Now he turned his head, his eyes wandering vacantly over the room. Tom could see the big hooked nose, the deep-sunken eyes, the cleft bulb of the big chin.

"Yes," Tom said, "that's C. M. Furnival."

The Rolls-Royce was facing the gates and in it Gordon Haines was as tense and as still as a cat preparing to pounce. Over the last minutes, after the conversation with Mrs Yorke about his sick friend, he had gradually come out of his fear-induced torpor and had began to burn with indignation. Beside him Lady Gamp and Cap ignored him, concentrating their remaining powers on survival. Ahead of him was Marbles's huge head. Gordon could not turn to see the house because the big oaf kept glancing in the rear-view mirror, on the lookout for the exit of his colleagues in crime. It was getting darker and darker, with heavy storm clouds coiling and changing shape like a collection of Monoraths.

There was a loud shout from the front of the building. "Oi! You! Get down from there!"

Looking up at the telephone wires the burly Sammy had seen Tom and Bess many metres above him. The shout galvanised Gordon and he wrenched open the car door and was running for the house before Marbles had time to do anything but echo, "Oi!"

Bess looked down; Tom was too petrified by the height.

Gordon Haines yelled at big Sammy, "Where's the Warden? I have to talk to her!"

Sammy grappled with the frenzied

publisher. "Oh no, you don't!"

Hearing the commotion beneath, C. M. Furnival got to his feet and staggered weakly to the window. Tom tapped on the glass and put on a pleasant face, indicating he wanted to come in. They stared at each other through the window. Bess cupped her hands to her mouth and called exuberantly, "Let us in! Go on!"

Slowly, oh so slowly, the author set his fumbling fingers to work on the window catch.

Sammy was not Marbles and really felt it when Gordon butted him in the stomach. He bent double and said, "Oof," and he said it again when Marbles accidentally knocked him over while chasing Gordon into the building.

Some of the staff were standing in the hall. They had been joined by the cook, a well-muscled man wielding a cleaver.

"Where's the head-woman?" Gordon shouted wildly.

Marbles bawled, "Mr Jackson! Travis!"

Sammy lurched in and rugby-tackled Gordon around the knees. Gordon struggled free and reeled into the wall. Finding his hand resting on a fire extinguisher, he wrenched the apparatus loose.

"Stand back!" he screamed. "These men are dangerous lunatics!"

Travis and Mr Jackson had arrived from the television room. "They're on to us!" Marbles bellowed to them.

"Everyone keep quite still!" came a ringing voice. Mrs Yorke stood there, steely-eyed, with a small glittering instrument in her hand: a hypodermic syringe.

For a moment there was silence. The staff began to edge towards their uninvited guests, cutting off the angles for escape in any direction. Mr Jackson murmured to Travis, "We still ain't got the man we came for."

"All is not lost," Travis said. He raised his voice. "Madam, you believe I am a medical man."

"No, I don't," Mrs Yorke said. "Not for a minute."

"Your second name must be Perspicacity." Travis beamed. "No, I am – as it happens – here on other business." He made his voice louder still. "I am an accredited agent of the Ministry of Health. We have reason to believe the kitchens here are serving up food containing mind-altering substances!" With that he promptly transformed to his Master Grievant wizard appearance and raised his staff to the heavens, booming, "Freeze, suckers!"

Unable to believe their senses, the nurses near him shrank back. Travis nudged Mr Jackson, calling to Marbles, "Come on!"

Marbles blundered after the other two as they ran up the old mahogany staircase.

"Stop them!" Mrs Yorke directed her minions. "It was some foolish party trick!"

But the three creations had a head start on their pursuers. Left behind were Mrs Yorke, Sammy and the cook.

"It's a vicious lie!" The cook was outraged. "Those sausages were only a week past their sell-by date."

Mrs Yorke advanced on Gordon and the fire extinguisher. "You're not well, Mr Haines. Put that down at once."

Gordon had his eye on the hypodermic in her hand. "Not till you put that down.

It's the others you want to stop. Don't you understand? I'm as clear in my head as you are!"

"You'd be the first who was," she said grimly and came nearer, with Sammy and the cook beside her. Behind them a tea trolley bounced down the stairs and crashed at the bottom, scattering items of stainless steel and tea from a giant urn.

Gordon bashed the fire extinguisher on its soft spot and the device spurted a clinging white powder. He waved it around until they were all layered in the stuff like a display in a Christmas shop window.

Mrs Yorke did not for a moment deviate from her purpose. Looking like a haughty Snow Queen, she walked remorselessly up to Gordon and sank the hypodermic needle into his left buttock, pressing down the plunger with a practised thumb.

"No!" he cried, swinging the empty extinguisher.

Mrs Yorke ducked neatly. Sammy said, "Oof!" and subsided unconscious to the floor.

Travis saw the hunters regrouping after their close encounter with the tea trolley which had been left so fortuitously at the top of the stairs. "You two to the left!" he ordered and ducked low out of sight to go the other way, calling in a low voice, "Mr Furnival! Where are you?"

Marbles and Mr Jackson, disappearing along the first-floor corridor, took up the cry, but much louder. Travis heard feet pounding to the top of the stairs and, resuming his modern appearance, slipped into the nearest room. The pounding feet went after Mr Jackson and Marbles. An old lady looked up from her embroidery. She wore a quilted dressing gown and had a ready smile.

"Hello," she said cordially. "Isn't it noisy today? Would you like a humbug?" She held out a tin towards him.

"Too kind, but no. Would you by any chance know the number of C.

M. Furnival's room?"

"The Furnace Room, did you say? I'm afraid I'm a little deaf."

"Ah. Well, I must be going."

"Lovely to see you, dear. Drop in any time. Bring a friend."

"Enchanting to meet you, madam."

Travis opened the door again and looked up and down the corridor. There was no one in sight but there was the most tremendous hubbub coming from the direction the other two had taken. After a second there followed a noise which Travis correctly interpreted as being the sound of a large number of people falling down the smaller, back staircase.

He went out of the room, waving an affable hand at the old lady. Shutting the door behind him, he had to admit that he was, for once, at a loss for what to do next.

A quiet voice said, "Travis. Here!"

He looked and saw young Tom by yet another stairway, which led upwards.

"Hello, young Tom! How did you get here?"

"Never mind. We've found Mr Furnival

– or, rather, Bess has."

"Well, how wonderful!" Travis went to him with a spring in his step. "Show me."

In the hall Gordon Haines fought furiously against the effects of the sedative injection. "You little fool!" he said to Mrs Yorke through clenched teeth as his legs gave way and he sat down heavily on the recumbent Sammy.

"Don't you talk to the Warden like that!" The cook was outraged on her behalf, but Mrs Yorke herself was impressed by Gordon's spirited battle to stay awake. Obviously the man had iron willpower, just as she had.

Gordon made a colossal effort and propelled himself to his feet. "I am attempting to prevent the abduction of C. M. Furnival," he croaked. "Help me!"

"These others – they're not friends of yours?"

"Far from it! They kidnapped me last night." He tried to stand upright without swaying. "If we could disable their vehicle, we might at least prevent their getaway." His legs buckled and he sat down again.

"Well, that is a most practical thought." It was Mrs Yorke's highest term of praise. "Let me help you."

In C. M. Furnival's room, Travis stared at his creator. "What, oh, what have we done to you?" he said mournfully.

The frail author worked his big jaw loosely and mumbled, "Know you, do I?"

Travis put a hand on his shoulder. "No. You never did. Otherwise you could never have made me a figure of fun."

Ever since he had let them in, Bess had not been impressed by the near-speechless, shabby old writer. She said forthrightly, "I'm not going back into *him*."

"Can we get on with it?" Tom demanded. "What am I going to say to my mum and dad if we get caught here?"

"I'm so sorry," Travis said. "Now, if I read it aright, that contraption is some sort of pulley thing."

He was looking at a device which was bolted to the wall above the window frame.

"Yes, I think it's a kind of fire escape."

"What a wise precaution!" Travis went

over and unhooked a canvas sling on the end of a long length of rope. "I assume it lets you down reasonably gently, though of course that would be if there's only one of you..."

"We can't all go at once – it wouldn't take it!" Tom stuttered with the horror he felt.

"Oh, be sensible, please! There's no time to go dropping it and raising it four times. And I thought you were bright!" Travis shook his head reprovingly.

"I'll climb down – how about that?" Bess suggested.

Travis smiled broadly. "There! Problem solved. So will I – and this thing must be able to take two if they're not heavy."

Tom was not so sure.

Cap and Lady Gamp sat in the Rolls with their backs to the mayhem going on in Branwell Nursing Home. They were clinging to life by a rapidly thinning thread. "They must hurry up . . . they will hurry up," Lady Gamp said dully.

"I don't like it," Cap moaned like a child. "I don't like it."

Supporting Gordon Haines with surprising strength, Henrietta Yorke emerged from the front door with the cook and his cleaver. "How do we do it?" she asked. "How do you disable a Rolls-Royce?"

"Distributor head," Gordon answered soggily and his knees buckled again. "We take it out."

In the house the chase had hotted up. A retired and outraged major from a tank regiment had organised some of the more active residents to assist in the task of harrying Mr Jackson and Marbles. They had fought a pitched battle in the kitchens, where the stew for lunch besmeared every surface, before the creations had been cornered in the dining room, where one solitary resident was eating an early breakfast with apathetic indifference to the shenanigans around her. Half concealed behind an upturned table, lobbing plates at the besiegers, Mr Jackson said irritably, "If we were allowed to let them get hurt, we could get out easy."

Marbles reminded him, "We can anyway. *We* don't get hurt."

Clinging to the waist of C. M. Furnival, who was trussed into the safety harness like an air-sea-rescue victim, Tom was descending the tower. The wind had died down and he could already feel moisture in the air. Above him Bess nearly managed to keep pace with them, almost scampering down the ivy.

At the window above, Travis held on to the rope, lowering it manually to be safe. Beneath him he saw three figures emerge into view, making unsteadily for the Rolls-Royce. The practical woman and a man with a cleaver were helping Gordon Haines . . . They were up to no good, for sure! His keen eye spotted the telephone lines which Bess had disengaged. Thinking of a good line for the brief journey, he jumped out into space, reaching for the wires.

"Geronimo!" Travis shouted.

Henrietta looked back at the house as two things happened almost at once. Two of the dining-room windows shattered. Marbles and Mr Jackson came through them as though fired from a circus cannon.

Before they hit the ground, she was aware of another moving object. This one came swinging from the sky clutching two wires like an elderly Tarzan on a jungle vine. It was the linen-suited conjuror. He hit the ground just after Marbles and Mr Jackson and, somersaulting, thereafter hit Gordon and the cook. Mrs Yorke grabbed at Gordon and went down hard herself.

Meanwhile Tom and C. M. Furnival were coming down at a highly accelerated rate. Tom shut his eyes. He would be maimed, or worse. . .

They landed in something hard and springy. Tom opened his eyes. They had been caught in the bulging arms of Marbles.

Marbles's face broke into a spontaneous smile of pure joy. "It's him," he said. "We got him!"

The long-threatened rain began emptying itself from the murky sky in buckets. Assorted staff and residents streamed out of the front door of the nursing home, led by the tank major, who trumpeted above the deluge, "This is an outrage!"

"Come on – leg it for the car," Mr Jackson said succinctly.

With Marbles carrying both Tom and C. M. Furnival, they reached the Rolls with little time to spare before the gates were blocked by a human wall. Bess had jumped the last six metres to the ground and sprinted to the car to open the doors for them. They all piled in as Travis began to drive. He aimed the huge car at the gates and missed by only a little, sideswiping one of them off its hinges. The Rolls Royce lost a headlamp and skidded sideways. Travis turned the wheel, driving in the direction of the skid, and corrected the drift. What a talent he had for these mechanical contraptions!

On the driveway, the retired major helped Mrs Yorke to her feet. In falling, the cook's cleaver had cut a heel off one of her shoes and she was lopsided in movement, but at least the storm had hosed them clean of the extinguisher powder.

"I'm disgusted, appalled! It's a disgrace," the major spluttered.

"Write to a newspaper about it," Henrietta Yorke said curtly and bent to haul Gordon to his feet. "Mr Haines – what next?"

"Get the police," the publisher said woozily. "Find a phone . . . Oh, heavens!" His legs gave way and with an involuntary gesture of affection he buried his head in her bosom.

Through the teeming rain Mrs Yorke could see her face reflected oddly in Gordon's bald head, and she watched herself say, "I've got a mobile in my car."

Struggling through the cascading rain, the estate car went up a long, steep hill with the engine working flat out. Inside, the travellers from Marshton Manor were agitated.

"I tell you," said Des, "this is the most dreadful world. What happens if we don't get back where we belong?"

"I'll be all right." Gloria ran a hand nervously through her hair and the car ran through the grass verge before she straightened the wheel. "I could make any man fall in love with me."

"You're not real, Glor." The Destructor was scornful. "What would any man want with you?"

"I could get by – that's all I'm saying," she said tersely. "I didn't say I *wanted* to stay here."

The Grey-Blue Man, whose energy and optimism seemed boundless, joined in the conversation. "I wanted to meet the Creator in this world, to shake his hand and to thank him!"

"What for?" Gloria asked cynically.

It only silenced the Grey-Blue Man for a

moment. "And to give him his mail," he added inconsequentially.

About a kilometre away, Mr Jackson was the only passenger in the front of the Rolls. The crush in the back seat was steamy and unendurable, largely because Marbles took up so much room. He had both Tom and C. M. Furnival on his lap, with the ageing author still in his safety harness; and Bess was wedged between them and the two invalids, Cap and Lady Gamp. Tom kept his head at an angle to stop it bumping on the roof. They were motoring flat out, going down a winding hill road. The wheels of the big car kept losing traction on the slippery tarmac, and they tore past a sign warning of flooding.

"Where are we? Where's the rest of them? What do we do now?" Mr Jackson was untypically worried.

"I'm heading for Marshton Manor," Travis said. "With any luck we should run into them."

And they did. The next moment everyone was shouting and Travis was braking and hauling at the steering wheel as they saw the estate car swinging wildly around a corner ahead of them. The Rolls spun violently, twice, before the two cars slewed sideways into each other in the middle of a deep puddle, throwing up a massive wave of mud and rainwater.

Tom's head met the roof of the Rolls with a weighty thud.

Chapter

When Tom woke up, he was lying in some kind of building looking up at the sky. His face was being washed by a lighter rain than had been falling earlier . . . and it was also being nuzzled by the Monorath. Pig-sized and slit-eyed, the monster pushed his beak affectionately into Tom's cheek.

"Sorry about this," came Bess's voice. "I

don't think he wanted Travis to get him out of you."

Tom said to the Monorath, "Do you mind," not too crossly, and sat up. He was at once dizzy and shut his eyes. "What's happening?"

"We're going back to the Creator. The Rolls was a bit of a write-off, so we got here in the other one. There's only one Grey Man left."

Tom sat up straighter and opened his eyes again. They were in some kind of disused barn. There was a smell of engine oil and old hay, sharp and dusty. Wooden beams like those in a church were exposed to the sky: most of the roof had fallen in long ago. The heavily dented estate car was over by the wide doors and Grandpa had his head under the bonnet. The remaining creations were clustered around Travis, who was holding forth in soft, compelling tones. Cap and Lady Gamp sat apart from them and with a shock of horror Tom realised that it was raining *through* them. The one Grey Man was kind of blue, he saw.

"Where's Mr Furnival?"

"In the car. I wish they'd get a move on."

Des, the most feared ruler in the history of Fortrain, looking dangerously un-solid, crawled over to them from the main group.

"Hi there," he whispered ingratiatingly. "Listen, Tim – you never really thought I'd torture you, did you? No, of course not. I'm all heart when you get to know me. Now: the thing is, the Creator's in bad shape. Very weak. We don't know if he'll take us back and survive the process. Then I thought, hey, there's young Tim – he reads a lot, I bet!"

"It's Tom."

"Whatever. What I mean is, you read fantasy stuff, don't you? Well – think of an author I could make my home in. Someone who's crying out for a dark and powerful character with charisma. Ideally a writer who lives pretty close."

"I can't help you," Tom said.

"And wouldn't if he could," Bess chipped in. "Anyway, you wouldn't make it. You look terrible, Des, what there is of you."

"It's all right for you – you're one of ones who's still got energy. Travesty-Warlock's got so much he reckons he can stay."

Tom became conscious that beside him the Monorath was swelling, fuelled by his loathing for the Destructor. Who said suddenly, "Gotta go," and scuttled back to the others.

"What did he mean about Travis?" Tom asked Bess.

"He thinks he can survive here on his own. I'd like to stay too, but I don't think I could keep it up. They're trying to talk him out of it."

Now the conversation in the main assembly was general and loud. Everyone was urging Travis and above them all Gloria helped coax him with shrieks of "Traitor, traitor, traitor!"

Travis stood and called out, "I bow to the majority. Anything to shut Gloria up. Now let's get on with it!"

Tom and Bess joined them and they all went to the car, where Marbles lifted out

Mr Furnival and gently laid him on the filthy floor.

The writer was completely inert and Mr Jackson had a frightening thought. "He's not dead, is he?"

Marbles shrugged. "Dunno. Never seen a dead man, have I?"

"What?" Des was aghast. "He can't be dead!"

Travis had knelt by the damp author. "He's not – only giving up. And I won't let him."

They all watched as the wizard in the linen suit lowered his head and gave his creator the kiss of life. He breathed into him at regular intervals, holding Mr Furnival's nose in the approved fashion. Eventually he sat back on his haunches. "He's breathing, anyway," he said. "But he's cold and wet and I don't know how much longer he can go on."

Des murmured to Tom, "There must be another author you can think of. A younger man, preferably."

"No!" Travis's voice rang like a trumpet through the old barn. "He gave us life and the debt must be repaid. The sick will go first. Then someone with strength and energy." He was looking at Marbles and the big man nodded.

Tom was left by himself as the creations gathered closer round the old man in the dressing gown. He heard Travis whispering into his ear and crept forward to hear how it was done – but too late. When Travis stood up there was the misty hole in the air lingering around C. M. Furnival's head.

"Cap?"

Mr Jackson went to pick up Captain Magnificent, Prince Bramnoc of the Royal House of Graemor, and placed him on Mr Furnival's chest. By now Cap weighed nothing, yet from what you could see of him he was at his most noble. His voice, like his body, was a ghost of itself as he said, "Wish me luck. And thank you, Travesty, for putting me straight."

Travis smiled at him. "We are brothers."

Aaah. Cap was gone, In through the Eyes.

"Stephanie." Travis beckoned and Mr Jackson brought Lady Gamp forward.

She said weakly, flickering slightly with the effort of speech, "I'm so glad you're coming. I know there may be no future for any of us in there, but we should be together. And don't forget that special bond between us, Travis, the feelings we – "

Travis edged her nearer the Creator. "Please, dearest Stephanie, no long speeches."

She disappeared, looking rather cross.

Travis said, "Marbles."

"Right-oh." The big man lumbered in to

take up position at C. M. Furnival's head. He looked over at Mr Jackson. "See you in a minute. I hope. . ."

"Yeah – catch you later."

After Marbles had vanished, disappearing whence he came, Travis looked closely at Mr Furnival. The author's eyes were open but he saw nothing.

"Oh, dear," Travis said. "That lot didn't do him too much good. I hope I haven't sent them to their doom."

And now Bess was tugging at Tom's sleeve. "Have you got a minute? We're having a little problem with our monstrous dweller in darkness. He had such a good time with you that he seems to want you both to spend more time together. I wonder if you could talk him out of it?"

The Monorath was being held by Mr Jackson and the Grey-Blue Man. Gloria had found a broken piece of glass and was using it as a mirror. She said carelessly to the Monorath, "Here's your friend – he'll tell you himself."

"Yes. . ." Tom said, still feeling a little dizzy. "Um, hi."

The rolls of flesh on the Monorath quivered with pleasure and his little red eyes lit up hopefully. He ground himself a little way towards Tom, churning up the muddy floor. Tom swallowed, stepped up to the creature and gently stroked his head between the eyes. The skin was hard and lumpy.

"The thing is . . . Well, I'd be happy if you stayed with me. I'm not allowed a dog because my parents say they're too much trouble, but . . . You see, everyone belongs somewhere, and I think really you belong with Mr Furnival. It's just one of those things. But I shall think of you, if that helps."

The Monorath looked sulky and jerked his head away.

"I did tell you," Bess said to him sternly. "Now get over there."

The roly-poly monster squidged over to join Travis, who was warming the Creator by rubbing him with an old sack. As the Monorath came into his eyeline, a trace of recognition illuminated Mr Furnival's face. He stared at the beast and then suddenly sat bolt upright.

"The Blumpy!" he screamed hoarsely. "No! It's the Blumpy!"

"Well, externally it's having quite an effect!" Travis remarked brightly. And then said to the Monorath, "Off you go now – go on!"

The misty circle of air had floated up to maintain its position by the author's head. The Monorath bent his squat neck around to look at Tom. The monster winked at him – definitely winked – and was gone.

The internal effect on C. M. Furnival was stupendous. He stared around for a second, wide awake, then got briskly to his feet and said indignantly, "What in heaven's name is going on here? I demand to know!"

Travis took him by the shoulders. "You are having a pleasant rest, Mr Furnival. Soon it will be time for tea."

In speaking, he had met and held the author's eyes, which dimmed again slowly, though he remained standing.

"Oh," he said limply. "Tea. Jolly good. . ."

He was passive again, staring into space.

Grandpa Blake called from the car, "What's happening over there?"

Travis called back, "Everything's absolutely fine, Arthur. Just tinker with the motor and don't worry about a thing."

Tom had the notion that Grandpa, his brain overtaxed already, was grateful for the chance to stay hidden under the estate car's bonnet.

Travis said sadly, "Awful shame about the Rolls-Royce, but the police would have had a description of it by now, anyway. Speaking of the need for haste, we'd better try a job-lot this time. Everyone all together. He seems up to it."

Strangely, now they had the evidence that their return was working successfully, he sounded depressed instead of elated.

Des expressed what he was thinking. "It won't be the same. Whatever happens, the glory days are gone. And how will we hold on to who we are, if he doesn't write any more books?"

"Did you have to put him under again

so soon?" the Grey-Blue Man asked peevishly. "I wanted to give him his mail, in person. It's the only real chance I'd ever have of meeting him."

"His mail? What mail?" Travis asked.

The Grey-Blue Man produced a single air-mail letter. "This. It's not much, but I thought if someone had taken the trouble to write, he'd like to have it as soon as possible. I know *I* would, if someone wrote to me."

Travis was staring at the envelope. There was a little logo in the top left-hand corner: TransWorld Pictures. "It's Hollywood," he said, ripping the letter from the envelope as he spoke. His eyes darted down the typed page.

"Gimme that!" Gloria squealed and at the same time Mr Jackson said, "What's it say?" and Bess asked, "Who's it from?" and the Grey-Blue Man said, "You mustn't open other people's letters."

"We are part of the Creator," Travis said pompously. "We have the right." Looking up, he placed himself in a shaft of light, and read the letter aloud.

234

I felt I had to write myself via my personal secretary because I just know we're going to get on. I'm flying one of our Vice-Presidents, Melvin Walsh, over to Britain and I hope you will be able to visit with him at the Dorchester Hotel within the week, along with your agent, publisher and legal adviser. The fact is, after it came up through the chain of command, I myself have read your book The Endless Darkness of Crowfar *and it has 'movie' written all over it. A young fan of yours wrote me about your work and Melvin hopes to meet him too. The designer Jonas Barton is in touch with the Welsh Water Authority (I think it is) about a location he's already found for the bottomless pit you mention in the book.*

I can't tell you how excited we all are here. Later I hope to get you over to my Nevada ranch to talk about merchandising, but that will have to wait until my wife and I are through with our divorce litigation which you will have read so much about. This motion picture is just going to be so

*good! I feel we are twins and a longer letter
follows from my lawyers.*

> *Warmly yours,*
> *Saul Goldman*
> *President in Perpetuity, TransWorld
> Pictures Inc.*

All was still in the old barn when Travis
had finished reading. Then Bess said quietly, "You did it, Travis! You really did it."

Gloria's voice was low and emotional
too. "I wonder who they'll get to play me?
And Cap? I've got to get back and tell him.
I've got some great scenes in that book!"

"There'll be more books now! Let's get
back," agreed Mr Jackson with shining
eyes.

"Bags I tell first — I was the one with
the letter!" The Grey-Blue Man joined the
other two jostling in on Mr Furnival,
who stood there like a statue. The three
of them vanished in the same instant,
leaving Mr Jackson's words hanging in
the air: "Yes, but you didn't want us to
open it. . ."

So then there was only C. M. Furnival standing there, slack-mouthed, and Travis, and Tom, and Bess.

Travis shot her a suspicious glance. "I hope I'm not going to have trouble with you, young Bess."

"No. I wanted to say goodbye to Tom."

"Ah, youth," Travis said sentimentally. "Do you mind if I watch?"

"Don't be stupid," Bess snapped angrily and then had nothing more to say. Feeling self-conscious, Tom held out his hand.

"Bye, then, Bess."

They shook hands slowly. Bess's grip was not as strong as it had been.

"Yuh. It was . . . it's been . . . um. See you later, then."

Travis was disappointed. "Is that it?"

Bess looked upset suddenly. "I think I hate

237

goodbyes." She hesitated, stepped back and vanished.

"Hopeless," Travis said regretfully. "An opportunity for a tremendous little scene, and quite wasted. Come with me, Tom."

They left C. M. Furnival standing in front of his hole in the air and went past Grandpa's legs (he was now working under the car) to where the big doors gaped open to the world. It was brighter than before outside, but still windy, with dirty clouds tearing across the steel-grey sky. The creations had picked a hide-out quite high up, among fields.

"Wonderful to be alive," Travis murmured. "Wonderful! You know, Tom, I wanted to deceive them. Get them all back and then stay. To be who I wish to be, beyond the reach of the man who made me . . . beyond the books. But I find one has responsibilities one cannot escape."

"Believe me, Travis, you get those here too. It's not all freedom and doing what you like. There's always things you've got to do and you don't want to."

Travis kept looking out over the wet rolling hills around them. Then he said briskly, "Well, now. The road down there goes straight on to the motorway. For getting back to Marshton Manor."

The practical consideration panicked Tom. "But – but . . . What do I say? What do we *say*?"

Feeling it did not concern him, Travis dismissed the problem. "Oh, use your imagination." He left Tom worried, staring out through the doors, and wandered back into the barn, speaking quietly the while. "There's so much one could have done. So much I'm going to miss. Think of it! The chance to control my own destiny – the possibility of . . . stripping down a hover-mower, to see how it works . . . tuning in to nonstop country-and-western music with the knowledge that I can change channels whenever I wish . . . Don't you see it?"

Tom turned round and could not see anything very well because the light in here was so much dimmer than outside. It took him several seconds to realise that Travis was no longer there.

AND FINALLY

The new house was just that: new. The persistent smell of fresh paint was a curious hindrance to reliving in his mind those heady times of a few months ago. . .

Mr Furnival's body had abruptly jerked and he was completely restored to himself, asking, "Who's that boy? Not a fan, I hope. I can't stand young people. Is that you, Arthur?"

For the next few minutes Grandpa had stuck to one simple line: "You're soaking wet. We must get you home. Time to talk later!"

Fortunately the author had dozed off in the car. Then, as they joined the motorway, Grandpa had said in an exasperated voice, "Well?"

Tom was ready for him. "We were kidnapped. Some strange people wanted to find Mr Furnival, and he wasn't at all well, but they didn't hurt him and he got better."

"Ah," Grandpa had said. "Yes. That's about what I remember of it too. And of course I had been getting those headaches – haven't been well myself, have I?"

"Not well at all," Tom reassured him. "I expect everything's a bit hazy."

"Very hazy. As a matter of fact, completely hazy. Yes. And, um, Tom . . . Best not tell your mother if we can help it. Eh? And being . . . *hazy* like this, we couldn't tell her much anyway, could we?"

"No," Tom had agreed solemnly.

Grandpa and C. M. Furnival had a long talk that afternoon – long for Grandpa, at any rate. Then Mr Furnival rang Gordon Haines. The upshot was that all three men claimed to have been asleep or drugged or both during the time they were held by what Gordon called the Fortrain Action Group. They agreed that none of them would press charges even if the miscreants were apprehended, and Mrs Yorke was silenced by a three-book contract from Gordon Haines, who told her anyone could do it if they could think of the right subject matter and he could help her out there.

C. M. Furnival was a rejuvenated writer and within a matter of weeks had completed a first draft of a tremendous new book –

although he himself was at a loss to explain why he had felt it necessary to make so many little changes to well-established characters . . . Sometimes he wondered where he got the ideas from!

In *The Twin Mountains of Olan* the Destructor had never had such quantities of Phratons and Grisemen at his disposal – and yet his hold over the Monorath was less certain than it had been. Prince Bramnoc was again wounded badly and this time did not make a complete recovery. He became king, a somewhat withdrawn, stately individual. Queen Gloriana took on the active side of things in the royal household and was seldom seen out of armour (the attractive filigree kind). Mr Furnival found that, against his better judgement, he was putting in too many references to her golden hair, which was for ever flowing behind her in luxuriant waves when she rode anywhere. She was assisted by a new character, a storming fighting man who wore silver-blue armour and had a passion for her, even to the extent where he described her as being 'lovely as the dawn'. (The mix of vim and naivety was typical of the Grey-Blue Man whom Tom had met briefly in the old barn.)

Mother Gamp mothered on energetically in a welter of indistinguishable stews and poultices, and the old author cunningly inserted a clue that young Bess might have a hidden past which could make her important in later stories.

Somehow Master Grievant had lost his comic touch after being elevated to the rank of High Sorcerer. However, he did have a new strength and dignity, and the comedy element (it occurred to Mr Furnival) could be given to Marblehead and Snorth (Son of Jax), who got up to all kinds of irresponsibility.

Tom never again had bad nightmares. It is true that he still had frightening dreams, but somehow even during them he was conscious that he was dreaming, which took the edge off them. The under-bed monster which had plagued him never returned. Although he had the vague suspicion that the Monorath had scared it away, Tom preferred to believe that it was his own growing confidence that had defeated the nightmares. He remembered how brave he had been, climbing the ivy of the Branwell Nursing Home, and marked it as a watershed in his development. Either way, it was a definite relief to be able to turn out the light without dreading sleep. He rather thought that in his own childhood C. M. Furnival had suffered from bad dreams, in which he had named his own private terror 'the Blumpy'.

Seated today at his desk in dank Marshton Manor, C. M. Furnival was experiencing a nightmare new to him. It was the twentieth draft of a film script entitled *The Endless Darkness*, which had just been sent to him 'personally' by Saul Goldman, whose energetic handwritten notes and doodles on the pages made the whole thing yet more grotesque. "What? What?" Mr Furnival said aloud, in mounting incomprehension. He had reached page 63, where:

SNORTH *gets hold of the gigantic* BIG GRISEMAN *and lifts him high off the ground.*

SNORTH

No one calls me small. Think you're big? Yeah? Yeah? Even bigger now, aren't you? Taller, huh? Well, brother, the bigger they come. . .

He drops the BIG GRISEMAN *into the Death Tube.*

CUT TO: INT. DEATH TUBE. NIGHT.

The BIG GRISEMAN *endlessly falling, turning, screaming.*

CUT TO: EXT. CLIFFS. NIGHT.

MUSIC – THE 'YOU'RE GONNA GET YOURS' SONG. *The* BIG GRISEMAN *shoots out of the hole in the cliff and falls to his death.*

CUT TO: INT. GRISEMAN PRISONS, TORTURE CHAMBER. NIGHT.

'YOU'RE GONNA GET YOURS' CONTINUES UNDER:

SNORTH
(turns from the death tube, grins)
. . . the harder they fall!

MARBLEHEAD *puts down his cigar and they exchange a 'high five'.*

MARBLEHEAD
Now – how much time we got before the bomb goes off?

CUT TO: INT. CAWNOR PALACE, GLORI-ANA'S BEDCHAMBER. NIGHT.

'YOU'RE GONNA GET YOURS' FADES, TO BE REPLACED BY THE HAWAIIAN GUITAR

LOVE MOTIF.
This is the first time we have seen the princess's bedroom. There are mirrors everywhere and heavy brocade curtains. The four-poster bed dominates the room. It's the kind of place you can smell perfume in just by looking at it.

GLORIANA *is sitting in her long white nightrobe, brushing her hair in front of one of the mirrors.* CLOSE-UP: *her lips are parted. She is thinking of the man she loves.*

– *And* BRAMNOC *bursts into the room. His tunic is torn clear down to his waist, revealing his blood-smeared chest, which heaves with pent-up emotions. How much can a man take – a real man like this one?*

BRAMNOC *(husky)*
Gloriana. . .

GLORIANA *(bosom heaves)*
Sir Prince – these are my private chambers. How – why – what . . .? Where is Master Grievant? He was guarding my door.

BRAMNOC *(steps towards her)*
He has taken too much wine.

GLORIANA
He would not do that. You have bribed Momma Gamp to slip him a posset.

BRAMNOC *(slowly getting closer)*
Honey, you can read my mind. Sure I did. Any man would do that and more to get close to you. Why fight it, baby? I know you want me like I want you.

GLORIANA *looks away. She doesn't want him to see the truth in her eyes — that she longs for him the way any woman longs for the man she loves. Suddenly* WE SEE HIM IN THE MIRROR *and he can see her eyes and she can see his and there can be no pretence between them. He grabs her roughly and spins her into his arms.*

BRAMNOC
No more words. I've loved you since that first day we went horse-back riding. Your face, your figure . . . I may be a prince, you may be a princess — but we're flesh and blood, aren't we? OK, so there's a war on. Does that mean two people can't —
She silences him with a long kiss. Outside Fortrain is going down the tubes but in here there is only love.

CM – I know what you're thinking. She's always brushing her hair – right? Don't worry! We're sticking her in a bath for this scene – what kind of milk would they have in it?

Appreciate your input at any stage. S.G.

C. M. Furnival could read no further. He was bewildered – horrified.

Then comfort came, from a strange source. There were faint voices sounding in his head. . .

A young woman who seemed to be American herself was saying, "They'll get a mega-star to play me. It's great – ooh – makes me tingle all over!"

An old man with a breathy voice like the sea in a shell replied, "It's nauseating rubbish, Gloria, and you know it. Should sell the books, though. . ."   END